Addicted
TO A DETROIT
SAVAGE
2

A Novel By

APRIL NICOLE

Royalty Publishing House is now accepting manuscripts from aspiring or experienced urban romance authors!

WHAT MAY PLACE YOU ABOVE THE REST:

Heroes who are the ultimate book bae: strong-willed, maybe a little rough around the edges but willing to risk it all for the woman he loves.

Heroines who are the ultimate match: the girl next door type, not perfect - has her faults but is still a decent person. One who is willing to risk it all for the man she loves.

The rest is up to you! Just be creative, think out of the box, keep it sexy and intriguing!

If you'd like to join the Royal family, send us the first 15K words (60 pages) of your completed manuscript to submissions@royaltypublishinghouse.com

ACKNOWLEDGMENTS

I dedicate this to God first, for you are the reason I wake up every morning. You are the reason I am alive and in perfect health. It was you that loved me first and gave your only begotten son to die for me, yet while I was still in my mess. It was you that gave me this talent and passion for writing. I am forever grateful for your goodness and mercy. Secondly, to all my supporters. Thank you all for encouraging me to continue to write. There were times I wanted to give up, but it was you all that kept me going. Without you all, I don't know what I would do. We all need a little support here and there. I am forever grateful for your support.

A special thanks to my little manager/daughter Aiyana. You are the reason why I hustle hard the way I do. To provide you with the life I never had. We gone make it out the hood, watch and believe. To my niece, Shanice W., for helping me proofread. Hopefully I can inspire you to be a writer. One day you will be able to write a story of your own. My sisters, all five of you—Nicole, Simone, Rita, Fatty, and Bipp —thanks for joining the hype. To my publishing company, I love y'all. F*ck them haters. I'm still standing. Thanks for answering my thousand and one emails, my late in the evening calls, and my persistent

text messages. To my editor, thanks for the corrections. My ass should have been paying attention in English class. If I was paying attention, half the shit I write would actually make sense. To my graphic designer for this dope ass cover art. My shit selling like hotcakes with this cover! Lastly, to anyone I may have missed, thank you all for all the reading and supporting that you do.

Rest peacefully Mom and Dad!

RIP Kobe Bryant/Gianna #24 MAMBA

SYNOPSIS

*O*h sh*t, things have just gotten really ruthless in the streets of Detroit. After Cali's gruesome murder, Kairo and Delano are now on the hush to cover it up. They receive an unexpected visit from someone who was presumed dead months ago, Johnny, and his return shocks them both as they find out he is not alone. Now Kairo and Delano must work diligently on keeping their secret while their relationship begins to unravel right in front of their eyes.

Once Kairo receives some shocking results, this puts the icing on her and Delano's relationship. She meets a new guy named Michael, but he is no knight in shining armor either. He will do anything in his power to keep Kairo in his life. King of manipulation is Michael's middle name, and there is no shame in his game. Kairo soon finds herself trapped in a love triangle with a fling that has a wild outcome. Now torn between the two, she must choose between Delano and Michael. Who will win Kairo's heart? Michael or Delano?

Meanwhile, Delano's life is left in shambles as someone comes forward with a shocking confession. Shit hits the fan when he finds out the truth about his roots, and this causes him to change significantly. If

you thought Delano was a savage before, wait until you see what he has become now. Will someone put an end to his reign? Or will he burn the entire city down along with the people in it?

PREVIOUSLY...

Delano noticed Kairo's Range was out front parked next to a black Charger and grabbed his heat from the glove compartment.

"Son, no matter what happens, stay in the car," Delano warned Malachi before getting out the truck. He crept up on his own porch and every single light was off. The only light he had was the moonlight. He noticed the door to his foyer was already ajar and pushed the door open completely, flicking on the lights. In front of him sat Kairo tied to a chair with tape over her mouth. As soon as he was about to run towards her, he felt a gun on his back.

"Nah partner, not so fucking fast!" a familiar voice said as he pushed the gun further in his back ushering him to move. As he walked slowly towards Kairo, Delano thought he could outsmart the man who had the gun. As soon as he turned, a bullet ripped right through Delano's shoulder.

"AAAAAAGGGGHHHHH!" Delano screamed as he felt the bullet pierce his right shoulder not exiting. He fell to the floor, looking up as if he'd seen a ghost as he looked in Johnny's face. Delano thought he

was dead. He watched him fall to the ground after he shot him multiple times.

"Remember me nigga?" Johnny said stepping on Delano's bloody shoulder.

"Alright Johnny, play nice. We need the nigga alive to find your sister," Johnny Sr. said walking into the living room. He was released early due to good behavior and now he was back looking for Cali. Johnny sat Delano up and tied him to the chair just like Kairo was.

"Delano, I find it clever of you and this bitch you call your fiancé to get rid of my daughter after she comes clean to you about my grandson, Malachi," Johnny Sr. said, blowing smoke into his face.

"Man, I don't know what the fuck you are talking about!" Delano yelled at Johnny Sr. He knew exactly what happened. It had been two weeks since Delano and Kairo killed Cali, but to Johnny Sr. and Johnny, she was considered missing. The last time they heard from her was when she gave them the address to Delano's residence. They were to seek her only if they hadn't heard from her, so here they were in the living room.

"I now have a missing daughter, Delano, and I have a feeling you may have killed her," Johnny Sr. implied. Although he was certainly right, he would never believe that until he recovered her bones.

"I haven't seen shit!" Delano yelled.

"Nigga don't talk to my dad like that." Johnny punched Delano in the rib cage just as he had done to him and Delano coughed. He thought Johnny was dead. Everyone thought he was dead, but he'd survived because he had on a bulletproof vest. He'd gotten shot twice but the vest caught the rest.

"Bitch, we know about your faggot ass. You're probably the reason Cali had HIV!" Delano retorted. Johnny Sr. and Johnny were both caught by surprise.

"What the fuck did he just say?" Johnny Sr. asked. He knew his son had better not liked dick. They both couldn't like the same thing.

"No, hold on." Johnny held his hand up at his father.

"What the fuck did you just say nigga?" Johnny asked again.

"I said, bitch-you-a-fag," Delano said slowly so the words could register in Johnny's head, upsetting him.

He took the gun and aimed it at Kairo's head.

POW! POW! POW!

"Don't play with me. Play with yo' b*tch." – Yo Gotti

OUT OF THE GAME

*B*ADUMP! BADUMP! BADUMP!

DELANO'S HEARTBEAT increased as he slowly watched the gun being pointed towards Kairo's head. His heart sunk immediately into the pit of his stomach. He did not know how this was going to end, but from the looks of it, it was not going to end well. He sat there in agonizing pain as he watched Kairo close her eyes and cry silently. Warm tears cascaded down her cheeks before Johnny pulled the trigger. *POW! POW! POW!*

The sound of his gun went off, firing three rounds into the glossy white wall behind her. Kairo's muffled screams filled the entire room, each bullet barely missing her head by an inch. She just knew she was out of the game, the same way she had taken Cali out, showing her no mercy.

Delano was at a standstill, frozen like the icecaps underneath the Antarctic Ocean. The thought of Kairo being shot in front of him was more than he could ever bare, and it made him fucking sick. He knew he wouldn't be able to handle seeing Kairo's brains all over the room.

After all, it was all their fault Cali was missing, but they were never going to admit that.

"Man, what the fuck!" Delano yelled. His heart was beating at a fast pace and he winced as he felt the sharp pain from his bloody shoulder where the bullet was lodged, but still visible. He looked up, fixed his eyes on Johnny and followed him as he came closer.

Johnny was breathing hard in Delano's face, clinching his jaw because he was petrified of what he knew. He didn't want to risk being exposed, for he was ashamed of being a homosexual. He blamed his father still, after all these years, never forgiving him for molesting him as a child.

"Nigga, the next bullet won't miss her! Say something else!" Johnny threatened as he turned the gun onto Delano, nudging the bottom of the barrel on his head. *I wonder what else he knows.* He was still thinking about how Delano knew about his secret. He couldn't help but to think it was Cali who snitched. After all, she did walk in on him having sex with her boyfriend.

"Man look, we don't have shit to do with Cali!" Delano implied, lying through his teeth.

Johnny Sr., finally having enough of Delano's bullshit, pulled out one of the chairs from the dining room table and sat down in front of him. He was determined to find out what happened to his daughter, and he was going to get to the bottom of it, even if he had to kill somebody himself.

"My son, I'm going to be straight anal. I think you know more than what you're telling us, so where should we start?" he held his cigar tightly in his hand as he looked at Delano with contempt.

Johnny Sr. always despised Delano, ever since he was a little boy. He didn't see what California seen in this arrogant ass nigga. It was one thing to fall in love with him, but another to get pregnant by his nothing ass. Johnny Sr. didn't know anything about the grown man,

he just remembered him being a weak little boy before going to prison.

"Start where? I already told you, I don't know what the fuck you are talking about," Delano was still playing that innocent role, but neither Johnny Sr., nor Johnny was believing nothing he was saying. That was Delano's truth and he was sticking to it. He didn't want to get Kairo killed, nor did he want to see the bottom of the Detroit River.

"Keep on playing with me! I know you know what happened to California. She sent a text message with your address to my son, now she is missing," Johnny Sr. accused, pointing his long slender fingers in Delano's face. He knew something was up, he just didn't know where to start.

"Are you deaf or fucking stupid? I just said I don't know what the fuck you are talking about. Cali was a crackhead-hoe. She's probably in Detroit sucking dick to get her next rock." He smirked, unaware that Johnny was going to pistol slap him.

"Nigga watch who the fuck you are talking to!" Thwack! Thwack! Johnny took the pistol and struck Delano across the face twice.

"Son calm down. We don't always need to resort to violence to get the answers we need." Johnny Sr. wasn't as hostile as he used to be when he was younger. He'd had a lot to think about while he sat in that prison cell day in and day out for 15years, and it taught him a lot of patience and endurance.

Johnny felt some type of way and asked,

"What the fuck you mean? This nigga tried to kill me and now my sister is missing. You gone tell me violence is not the way to handle anything? Why is this nigga even still breathing?"

He was in his feelings and he had every right to be because he was right. Delano did try to kill him and helped with killing Cali as well, but Johnny didn't know that. Most importantly, Delano knew his

secret. That was more of motive to silence him, but Johnny wanted to find Cali first.

"Son let me talk to you for a minute." Johnny Sr. led Johnny outside by the pool where they keep the other staff bounded as hostages.

This was the perfect time for Delano and Kairo to try and free themselves. They began loosening their ropes, but it was too challenging to get the knot untightened. By the time Delano caught a break by reaching a loop in the knot, the bodyguards were sent in from the pool to watch over them.

Malachi was still outside waiting inside the truck. He was listening to Kendrick Lamar's entire *DAMN* album through his new Air Pods on his iPhone11. He looked at the time and realized it had been forty-five minutes to an hour since Delano had told him not to get out. He never once came back to check on him. Then he suddenly got a vibe that something was not right. *What if he ran into some trouble?* Malachi thought as he exited the truck. He walked over to the black Charger and looked inside the windows spotting a handgun on the passenger seat.

He then retrieved a wire hanger from one of his bags and used his professional car thief skills to obtain the gun without setting off the alarm. Malachi was trained to use a gun, no matter the size. He knew how to aim and to be precise with it, so he really wasn't worried about anything, as long as he figured out what was going on.

Creeping up to the front door, he could hear distinct voices coming from inside. The first thing he noticed was Kairo being tied up to a chair. She spotted him sneaking in and he advised her to be cool and not give his position away.

POW! POW!

He took the handgun, shooting both of Johnny's bodyguards, one by one. Johnny and Johnny Sr. ran back inside once they heard the gun shots and discovered both bodyguards had been shot.

Malachi pointed the handgun at them, and Johnny pointed his back. Johnny didn't give a fuck how old he was, if he was old enough to shoot, then he was old enough to take a bullet. Johnny Sr. just stood there watching Malachi walk into the living room. This was his first time seeing his grandson.

"My son, who taught you how to aim with such precision?" Johnny Sr. asked, impressed with Malachi's skills. Delano was also impressed. He continued to work on trying to get the knot loosened as Johnny Sr. was distracted.

"I'm not here to talk old man," Malachi replied, still walking towards him.

"Why are they tied up?" He nodded towards Kairo and Delano.

"We're looking for someone. Her name is California Jones. Do you know who she is?" Johnny Sr. asked while pulling a picture from his back pocket and holding it up so that Malachi could get a good view of her.

"She is your mother."

"Nah, I don't know who that is, but can y'all let them go before it gets ugly?" Malachi threatened. He had never met Cali in person, but he knew she was his biological mother. They only communicated through mail because his adoptive parents didn't want to expose him to her lifestyle.

"Is that a fucking threat little nigga?" Johnny positioned his gun in the middle of Malachi's chest. Johnny didn't care if Malachi was his nephew or not, he was about to take him out.

"I guess we will have to wait and find out!" Malachi didn't flinch. That tough shit didn't faze him for one second. He might have been tall and slim, but he wasn't no punk bitch. He just stood there and let Johnny talk his shit, turning his face to the side avoiding Johnny's foul breath that was blowing.

"Johnny! No need to hurt our family," Johnny Sr. said putting his hand on Johnny's chest to calm him down.

"Fair enough. We will be on OUR way, but Delano if you hear anything from Cali, don't hesitate to contact me. My son, you are more than welcomed to leave with us."

"He ain't going no fucking where with you! AHHHH!" Delano yelled as the pain soared through his shoulder.

Malachi scoffed, looking at the two dead bodies that were lying in a pool of blood on the floor.

"Aye, good looking my nigga, but I don't know y'all and y'all leaving your trash behind."

"Man, fuck those bodies! Burn them!" Johnny retorted as he followed behind his father, getting inside the black Charger to leave. Malachi shook his head in disbelief. He couldn't believe they didn't give a damn about those men's lives. Obviously, they didn't give a fuck about nothing else but finding Cali, which was going to be no time soon.

"Aye, who were those people?" Malachi asked. He recalled the older man saying they were family.

"I promise to tell you when I get loose. You think you can help remove these ropes?" Delano winced in pain as his shoulder leaked blood profusely.

"Alright."

"Mmmm!" Kairo mumbled. Her eyes were blood shot red from all the crying she'd done, and the black coal from the mascara ran down her face.

"I got you!" Malachi removed the tape from her mouth slowly, being careful not to hurt her. Then he went outside to free the staff that was bounded by the pool.

Delano grabbed his bloody shoulder as he looked for supplies in the medical cabinet in the pantry to remove the bullet. Blood was now dripping onto the $5,000 a slab wooden floor.

"Baby, we got to get the fuck out of here. How the fuck is that nigga even still alive? We need to move as soon as possible!!!" Kairo expressed. There was no way in hell Johnny should have had the location to their home. Plus, she thought he was dead, so how could he possibly be there, alive in the flesh?

"Baby, you seen it for yourself. I killed him right in front of you," Delano responded as he handed her the supplies to help remove the bullet.

"I saw him hit the ground," Kairo responded sarcastically.

"I need you to be still because this is going to hurt a little."

"AHHHH!" he yelped in pain, but Kairo removed the bullet within seconds.

She put the bloody bullet in the sink and patched Delano's shoulder with gauze to stop the bleeding. Then she began to reminisce thinking back on that night. She was now regretting pulling the trigger.

"Ahhh, let it go you bitchhhh!" she yelled as she tussled with Cali for the gun.

POW!

She froze as she watched Cali slowly open her mouth. Delano pushed her off Cali, making sure it wasn't her that had gotten shot.

"Ah, helppp meeee!" Cali said weakly, laying down reaching out for help. She was choking and gasping for air as she bled to death on their patio.

"No help from me bitch!" POW! She fired a shot into Cali's skull, taking her out her misery.

"Baby, what the fuck!!" Delano said, grabbing his head.

14

"Help me get this bitch in the car!" she demanded as she took the dining room curtains and wrapped Cali's bloody body up with them. Delano helped load her body into the back of his white 2020 Lincoln Navigator and drove down to Detroit. They wanted to make sure Cali's body never come back identifiable, so they placed her on the train tracks and waited until the next train came. The train shredded her, cracking every bone in her entire body. Then they picked up what remained of her body and disposed it into the Detroit River. By the time someone found her, the body would be decomposed. Afterwards, Delano poured gasoline all over his truck and set it on fire, destroying anything that could possibly link them to Cali's murder.

"Hasta luego!"

"Baby, are you ok?" Delano asked interrupting Kairo from her thoughts. He'd seen the fresh tears rolling down her cheeks as she cleaned up.

"Huh?" Kairo sniffled, washing her hands in the kitchen sink. She didn't know Delano saw her crying.

"I asked if you're ok?"

"Hell, fuck no! Johnny, who is obviously still alive, was ready to kill us tonight! You should have seen the fire in his eyes!" Kairo gulped her glass of water she'd just poured to calm her nerves.

"I will handle it. I promise I will call—"

"Delano please. You're about as pussy as they come. You're always talking about how you're gone do this and that, but shit is always back firing on us. It's because of your stupid ass we are even in this position," Kairo said pissed. She thought back over her life and how things were so simple before they reconnected.

"Now, you hold on right there! We are in this together! Don't you go pointing the fucking finger on me!"

"Oh, it wasn't me that stuck my dick in that poisonous bitch because I don't have one! Anyway, where is Malachi?" Kairo asked. She wanted to be careful not to put the HIV business in his ear. As soon as Delano began to open his mouth to speak, Kairo gave him that *you better not* eye as Malachi walked in.

"Here I am, but who were those people?" he questioned again.

He was unaware that Johnny was his uncle and Johnny Sr. was his grandfather, but that was something Delano was going to have to eventually tell him. In order to avoid arguing with Kairo, he decided this was the time to tell him.

"Listen, let's talk about that while we get rid of these bodies," Delano said putting his arm around Malachi's neck and walking out the kitchen. He knew his son was capable of handling what was going on. If he was going to be living with him, Malachi would have to get used to seeing dead bodies as well as getting rid of them.

"I'ight, let's do this then," Malachi said helping his father dispose of the two men. He was not afraid, and confidently helped without hesitating.

Meanwhile, while they were busy talking and getting rid of the bodies Kairo grabbed a bucket of Ammonia and helped the staff clean up the pool of blood that was in her living room. She scrubbed in a circular motion trying to get up as much blood as she could, but the floor was stained from the blood that sat there, which was a constant reminder that someone died right in that spot. Her once beautiful home, went from being beautiful, to now being haunted by bad memories. Those were the memories she didn't want to keep. She'd had more flashbacks about Cali's murder than her own rape.

"What time is it?" Kairo asked herself looking down at her Apple watch.

"Oh shit, I got a shift tonight. Fuck that. I'm gone have to call off!" It was no way in hell she could work her shift at Beaumont under that kind of pressure.

Once Kairo finished scrubbing the blood off the floors, she took a hot shower and laid down in the bed. Thinking back over the years, she really thought Cali was her friend, but she found out the truth. She just wished she could have found out sooner than later. This whole possibility of having HIV ate at her conscious and she was afraid to get tested. She and Delano made an agreement to not get tested unless they were together, and they had yet to go because of fear that their chances would be high.

"Damn you!" Kairo screamed pulling the covers over her head before going to sleep. She hated she had to be the one to pull the trigger, but she was doing what she felt was necessary. At the end of the day, she felt Cali had gotten the death she deserved. She couldn't be trusted, so she took her out the game.

OPEN THE GATES OF HELL

"**O**pen the gates of hell!" TJ said to himself as he reached his destination. He stared at the address Johnny Sr. had given him on a piece of paper to confirm he was where he needed to be. He walked up on the cracked cemented stairs and anxiously knocked on the door of Johnny's home.

Knock! Knock!

Fuck! It's colder than a motherfucker! TJ thought to himself as he shivered from the cold breeze the winter was blowing through the Detroit streets. He knew he was wrong to come outside in the middle of the winter wearing some damn speedo leggings and a pink jacket with some brown UGG boots. Johnny finally arrived to answer the door in his long, warm, thick velvet robe with white fur trim around the collar.

"Can I help you?" Johnny asked leaning his head out the glass panel door, wondering why this man was knocking on his door like he was the damn police.

"Uh, is this the residence of Johnny Black?" TJ looked at the small piece of paper Johnny Sr. sent with him. He spoke slowly to make sure he had the correct name.

Johnny's facial expression changed and one eyebrow raised up.

"That's me? Who sent you?"

"See, I'm TJ, Cali's best friend and she text me two weeks ago with your name and address—

"Ok, AND?" Johnny said interrupting TJ from talking. He knew he was on some bullshit, plus he was annoyed by this bright flamboyant man flipping his weave back like some bitches do when they think they are just too cute.

"No, un, un. No need to be rude hon'tee." TJ shook his head lightly while moving his index finger side-to-side.

"I'm looking for my best friend. She sent me your address and name. Have you seen her?"

Johnny stood there trying to figure out why in the hell would she send this nigga a text with his information attached to it.

"My bad," he uttered from his lips, "but I'm looking for my sister as well and she would not be here."

"Wait! Are you even going to invite a bad bitch in? It's freezing cold out here!" TJ complained with his arms folded across his chest. Johnny reluctantly agreed, stepping aside and letting TJ in. The wind was so strong you could hear it brush up against the windows in the living room. Johnny had to move into a lowkey house on the West off Joy Rd, while his father moved into his mansion taking over the drug trade. That's how he knew TJ was on some bullshit about Cali giving him the address because she didn't know where he currently resided.

"Yea, we've been looking for her ourselves. Do you find it a bit strange that she isn't answering her phone?" Johnny asked, as he led TJ into the living room to sit down on his comfy grey couch.

"No, what I find strange is how you don't offer me a cup of hot tea or water. A bitch is real thirsty around these parts." TJ dramatically rolled his eyes and tooted his lips up after applying MAC's Pink Frost glossy lip gloss. He was demanding his hospitality and didn't have a clue that Johnny could take him out just by a single blow to his skull.

"You are really demanding as hell. Does your man spoil you like this?" Johnny said. It was pretty obvious he was gay because of his posture, the way he spoke, and that damn nappy ass wig he wore as a hat.

"Excuse me?" TJ turned his head sideways with his hand over his chest.

"You're reaching. You already don't want to let me in and don't want to offer me a drink, now you're questioning my sexuality?" TJ was slightly offended, but Johnny didn't see how when it was completely true.

"Dude, you came strutting your ass on my doorstep asking about my sister, being demanding and shit. How about you come suck my dick!" Johnny snared at TJ.

TJ put his right hand over his chest appalled. He was not expecting Johnny to snap at him like that.

"Oh ok. I'ma just go and come back when you're in a better mood." TJ got up to leave walking into the hallway.

"You know if you ever want your dick sucked, I could do that too. You might need some release in your life."

As soon as TJ put his hand on the doorknob, Johnny came up from behind and grabbed his face kissing him. Johnny needed some action. He was long overdue because the females weren't giving him that thrill; that thrill he so desperately needed with a man that could make his orgasm shoot through the roof.

TJ was caught by surprise as he continued to sloppily kiss Johnny back. He was full of surprises today. He felt like he needed to knock on random niggas' doors more often to get this kind of treatment.

Johnny was full blown gay. No woman could get his dick as hard as a man could. He would try to fight the urge of being gay and have sex with women, but he found his dick getting flaccid after they took their clothes off. He would stroke to get back hard, but his dick would go limp as soon as he entered their pussy. So, Johnny just gave up on trying and continued to jerk his dick while watching gay porn. Don's disappearance really fucked him up, so he had to jerk off to avoid getting blue balls.

TJ pulled down his Speedo leggings, allowing his elephant trunk of a penis to roll out. Johnny's eyes widened as he saw this enormous penis on such a small, skinny man.

"What's the matter? Big things can't come in small packages?" TJ teased as he slowly stroked his dick to its full capacity of length.

"No, it's perfect," Johnny said as he got on his knees and kissed TJ's balls before kissing the tip of his penis.

"Let's go back into the living room." They left out the hallway they stood in.

"Show me what that mouth can do," TJ said as he playfully smacked Johnny in the face with his dick. Johnny opened his mouth so wide, a herd of flies could have flown in. TJ was impressed with him and couldn't wait to see what Johnny's throat had cooked up.

Johnny licked around the base of TJ's dick up to the tip, producing a large amount of spit before spitting on the tip of his penis. TJ's pink press on nails began to pop off one by one as he held onto Johnny's head tightly while he received the best head he'd had in years. Johnny sucked on TJ like a brand-new Bissell vacuum cleaner, while he spread his skinny legs on the arm of the grey sofa.

"Oh, shit baby, you gone make me cum!" TJ screamed in his feminine voice. Johnny stopped and got up so he wouldn't cum just yet.

"What's the matter? Why you stop?"

"Bad girls don't get to cum until I say so!" Johnny slapped TJ across the face, pushing him back over the sofa arm. He was intrigued by this behavior. He'd never had a nigga toss him around like a rag doll before. "

Come suck this dick until I tell you to stop."

TJ immediately got on his knees and opened Johnny's velvet house coat. He was disappointed to find out Johnny's dick wasn't as big as his, but it was average enough to suck and fuck. Johnny's dick was already dripping pre-cum before it was even touched.

"My goodness, I got you dripping already nigga!" TJ opened his mouth and began to suck all of Johnny's problems away, making him groan as he'd just received some of the best head of his life.

"Ahhh, don't stop until I cum in your mouth," Johnny demanded as TJ deep throated him. It didn't take him long before he busted his nut down his throat. TJ was used to the taste of nut, so he swallowed him without hesitating. He kept sucking his dick as Johnny's body was still shaking from that enormous nut he'd just busted.

"Alright nigga, stop before I piss in your mouth."

"Gone right ahead!" TJ said opening his mouth to receive his golden drink. This turned Johnny on so much, his dick sprayed piss everywhere.

"Oh, shit nigga! Oh Shit!" Johnny yelled, as his piss squirted all over TJ's face. He then got up off his knees soaked from the golden shower Johnny had just given him. Johnny's heart was pounding so rapidly. It had been a while since he'd felt like this.

"Is there anything I can give you? You did a real good job relieving me."

"Actually, there is something you can do for me," TJ said stroking himself.

"You can make me cum."

"Right, but I'm talking about money wise," Johnny said. He wasn't ignoring TJ's request to return the favor, he just thought TJ would ask for anything else besides a nut. TJ straightened his clothes that now reeked of Johnny's piss.

"What I want, you can't afford to give me!" TJ snapped his fingers. It was then when it dawned on Johnny that TJ was clueless to who he was. Johnny chuckled, touching his freshly manicured goatee.

"For you to say that, you have no clue of who I am do you?" Johnny reached into his pocket and pulled out a stack of 100's equaling $10,000 and TJ's eyes lit the fuck up. Watching Johnny counting hundreds was making his dick hard.

"No, who are you?" TJ smiled twirling that synthetic matted ass wig. He lied. He knew who Johnny was all along. He just had to play his role and not fuck it up.

"WELL, if you don't know who I am, then it's best you don't know," Johnny said as he peeled off three crispy hundreds off the top and handed them to TJ.

"Take this, go get your nails done for real, get yourself a new human wig, and buy some new clothes. You stink of my piss."

"Damn, I should come over here more often!" TJ squealed as Johnny handed him the crispy hundreds. He forgot about wanting to cum and thought about all the fun he was about to have with Johnny down the road. He was glad he was sent knocking at his door because now he had a new sheriff in town. His dick was average, but from the looks of it, Johnny's money was long.

"Do you have a man?" Johnny asked. He was about to start a new DL relationship with TJ if he could abide by his rules and not fuck up.

TJ nodded his head no.

"Nope. Why do you ask?"

"I want to start something with you, but you have to be discreet about it. I'm willing to pay you ten grand a month if you make me cum on a regular basis," Johnny proposed to TJ. This was an offer that TJ just couldn't refuse.

"That's it? All I have to do is make you cum?" TJ asked to be sure. With ten grand a month, he would have more than enough to get his sexual reassignment surgery.

"Well Johnny, you got yourself a deal." TJ shook Johnny's hand and left.

"See you tonight at 8pm. Be ready," Johnny said closing the door behind TJ.

Now that Johnny had a new sex partner, that was the least of his worries. He now had to worry about his father coming to take the Detroit drug market from under his reign. He was determined not to let his father take over what he'd established while he was locked away in prison.

Growing up, Johnny never had the best relationship with his father. All Johnny wanted was to be normal, but how could he be normal when he was sexually attracted to men? He really hated himself, but it was a part of the man he had become, all because his father was on some pedophile shit and didn't protect him or California from the pedophiles, he called friends.

Johnny examined himself in the mirror, looking at his body that was still healing from the two-gun shots that Delano hit him with. Both bullets missed the main artery that could have cost him his life. He was still alive. After he changed his bandages, he looked in the medicine

cabinet reaching for his medication. Johnny was also HIV positive, but he made sure to take his medicine daily so that he would not infect the next person. He paid top dollar for his medications, not knowing that his meds weren't really effective, and he still was infecting people. That's how Cali got it from Don, and Don got it from Johnny. Now TJ would also have it as well.

He ran the shower as hot as he could stand it, stepping inside allowing the hot water to wash his sins away. He found himself scrubbing his dark skin until it became sensitive to the touch. He began to wail and cry in the corner of his shower, thinking about how his life was beginning to crumble in front of him. He'd done so many fucked-up things that God would never be able to forgive him.

RING! RING!

Johnny's house phone rang until he got out the shower to reach the cordless headphone on the bathroom sink. He looked at the caller ID and saw that it was a private call. It could either be a bill collector or someone playing on his phone, either way he decided to answer.

"Hello?" Johnny spoke plainly into the receiver.

"Son, what are you doing?" Johnny Sr. asked.

"I'm in the shower. What's up?" Johnny slightly caught an attitude. He was upset that his dad had taken over his mansion while he had to sleep inside a rental property.

"Hurry up and get your ass East. I'm calling an emergency meeting," Johnny Sr. said before hanging up the phone in Johnny's face. He was so angry that his father got granted for parole. He was gone kill that bitch ass lawyer he had for getting him released early. It was only a matter of time before he caught him slipping.

He returned to his shower letting the hot water run cold before getting out. He stood back in front of the mirror, picked up the clippers from the sink, and shaved his dreads off completely giving himself a low-cut fade. He trimmed up his edges leaving a crispy hair line and shaped his

goatee so smoothly you would think he went to the shop to get trimmed up.

He then walked over to his closet, picking out a fresh pair of black Levi's, a plain white tee, and his wheat Tims. Drenching himself in his favorite cologne Body Kouros by YSL, he put on his gold chains and his Cartier Buffalo horns and headed out to the East side of Detroit.

Johnny couldn't wait to see TJ again tonight. He knew that was the only person who would be able to take all this stress away. He planned on going to hear what his father had to say and then dip 30 minutes later to pick up TJ. When he arrived at his location, there were other trucks that Johnny didn't recognize. He assumed it was his father's friends.

"GET THE FUCK OUT RIGHT NOW!" Three men came rushing up on Johnny with their guns pointed at his head. He tried to reach for his handgun, but Malachi had taken it from the glove compartment.

TRRSSSSSS! The sound of glass shattered from the men shooting at the side window. It was too late. Johnny had driven to his own ambush.

RESULTS

*K*airo waited patiently for the results of her HIV test to return. She was a nervous wreck biting her nails and rocking like a drug addict. She knew they agreed not to take the test without each other, but this was eating at her conscious each day. She didn't know who to call but Delano and she was rocking on shaky ground. In her mind she tried to process where the fuck she went wrong for him to cheat on her like this. He could have had any other bitch in the world, but he had to choose Cali. Kairo got up off the examination bed and paced the floor. She was so nervous her body temperature skyrocketed like she had a fever.

Knock! Knock!

"Yes!" Kairo answered nervously as she turned around quickly after being startled when the doctor knocked on the door.

"I apologize. Did I startle you?" Dr. Michael Kramer asked, closing the door behind him. He was one handsome white man. He had blonde hair, blue eyes, and was slim and tall like 6'3.

"Oh no! It's ok." Kairo sat back down on the examination bed. Dr. Kramer pulled up a chair and scooted it closer to her. He took a deep breath before he could read her results.

"Before I tell you your results, you need to know that you could be terminated effective immediately if you are HIV positive," Dr. Kramer warned Kairo. She just nodded her head looking away.

"Have you recently had any symptoms related to this?"

"No, I haven't, nor have I bothered to read and find out," Kairo replied as the tears began to escape from her eyes.

"Well this is what I can do for you, if you are positive then I will discard your results and you don't have to worry about the board ever finding out. That's if you do this one small thing for me of course," Dr. Kramer said trying to bribe Kairo.

"What is that?" Kairo asked wiping her nose with the tissue.

"I will tell you after I read the results." Dr. Kramer opened the results.

"Man Kairo, I'm sorry but you are HIV positive."

"GOD DAMMIT! THAT MOTHERFUCKER!!!!!!" Kairo screamed.

Her reaction was ridiculous. She got up and threw things around the room; whatever she could find. Dr. Kramer had to take cover and warn the nurses out in the hall that Kairo was having a moment. It really wasn't much for her to throw around in that room except some supplies and chairs. Kairo finally calmed down and Dr. Kramer returned to the room.

"Are you alright?" he asked helping her straighten up the room.

"Hell, fuck nah I ain't alright!" Kairo snapped.

"I could possibly lose my life soon."

"No! Listen to me, you are stronger than you think you are. Don't settle for that bullshit because I will get you the best meds in town!" Dr. Kramer held onto Kairo while gazing into her beautiful eyes.

"What about my job?" Kairo asked, looking back into Dr. Kramer's blue eyes.

"All I want you to do is go to dinner with me tonight," he said.

"Dinner? You just found out that I'm HIV positive and you're asking me to dinner?" Kairo responded remorsefully. She'd just found out this terrible news and here this white man was asking her out to dinner.

Is he fucking crazy? Kairo thought to herself.

"I just want you to feel special that's all!" Dr. Kramer said not taking his blue eyes off her for one second.

"Ok, I will go with you and you promise to protect my job?" Kairo asked.

He nodded yes, pinky squared her, and winked his eye.

"I promise your secret is safe with me. I'll pick you up at 8," Dr. Kramer said as he took Kairo's cell number and left out the room.

Kairo dialed Delano's number immediately and got the voice mail. She was heated and needed to blow some steam off, so she called The Black Stallion. The staff said he was in a meeting and couldn't answer the call. Kairo climbed inside her truck and did 80 to 100mph all the way to the Eastside. Fuck the police, she was about to blow some shit up today. She pulled up in less than 20 minutes, parking in a no park zone.

"Ma'am you can't park there!" the valet guy said running up to Kairo. She pulled her Taser from her purse.

ZAAAAPPPPP!

"Back the fuck back!" she warned as she pushed the button on the side, causing the Taser to go off. He stopped running towards her, then

turned around and went back to his booth. Kairo kept walking until she approached Hailey, Delano's shift manager.

"Hello Mrs. Harris. Delano is in a meeting. I thought someone told you?" Hailey said trying to stop Kairo from fucking shit up. Kairo ignored Hailey and kept walking until she got into the kitchen. She looked for the sharpest butcher knife the club owned.

"Bitch, my name is Kairo and if you don't want to get cut and lose your job, you better get the FUCK OUT MY FACE!" she yelled. Hailey decided she didn't want that drama, so she stepped aside and let Kairo go.

She walked straight to Delano's office downstairs with the knife in her hand. He was indeed in a meeting, but Kairo didn't give a fuck about none of that! He'd given her HIV and she was about to fucking stab him. She finally made it to the room where Delano was with the others.

BOOOOM!

Kairo kicked the door in.

"BITCH YOU GAVE ME HIV!" Kairo yelled while running towards Delano who was sitting at the end of the table with a look of awe on his face. He was caught by surprise with Kairo barging in like this. She clutched the butcher knife in her hand tighter and stabbed him in that same shoulder he was shot in a couple of days ago.

"AGGGGHHHHH! WHAT THE FUCK!" Delano hollered as the butcher knife plunged deep into his shoulder blade. He pushed Kairo off him abruptly, sending her ass flying across the room like a damn rag doll. Everyone who was in the room with him gasped with their hands covering their mouths and ran out into the hallway.

"I'm sorry y'all, my fiancé and I have some business to attend to." Delano apologized and slammed the door in their faces. He diverted his attention towards Kairo who was now up and, on her way, to slap him.

"Kairo what the fuck are you—"

She slapped Delano so hard his bottom lip was hanging after spit flew across the room. He was now confused because he thought they'd made a deal not to get tested without each other.

"YOU FUCKED THAT BITCH RAW!!!" Kairo screamed as she tightly balled up her fist hitting Delano as he continued to hold his bloody shoulder.

"Kairo, it wasn't even like that! We never fucked raw, but we came close to it one time! I promise it wasn't like that," Delano confessed. For the longest he denied the fact that he had anything going on with Cali.

"You are lying sack of shit!!! It's over! Kairo removed her $50,000 engagement ring and threw it at him.

"I'm moving the fuck out!" She left Delano there bleeding as he reached out for her.

"KAIRO! KAIRO!" Delano called out her name, but she ignored him and kept on walking.

She left him standing there in his own pool of blood and didn't look back. She walked out The Stallion with his blood on her scrubs causing the staff to gasp. The EMT's rushed past her without bothering to ask if she was alright. They didn't know whose blood was on her. It could have been her own, but they kept going. *Fucking idiots!* she thought to herself as she climbed into her truck and pulled off in a hurry. She smiled as the tears fell heavily down her face into her lap. This was the tip of the iceberg. Their relationship was now over. The only good thing that came from all this chaos was that she didn't sell her condo. She could still go to it whenever she felt like it.

As soon as she walked in the front door, she took her scrubs off and threw them away along with everything he'd ever bought or given her, from designer bags and designer shoes, to expensive jewelry. She took a hot shower, put on some Jill Scott, and poured herself a glass of

wine. She was about to live her life like it was golden, not letting her HIV status determine her future.

Bzzzz! Bzzzz! Bzzzz!

An unknown number flashed across the screen of her phone from a West Bloomfield area code. She'd forgotten about her date with Dr. Kramer just that quick because she didn't think he was that serious about taking her out to dinner.

"Hey Kairo. This is Michael Kramer from Beaumont." He spoke smoothly and professionally like they were at work.

"Ahem, ahem." Kairo cleared her throat and then proceeded to say,

"Yes, hello. I forgot we are supposed to be going to dinner. I didn't think you were serious."

"Yes, I am very serious. You think you could be ready in 30 minutes?" Dr. Kramer asked.

"Yes, I will be Dr. Kramer," Kairo said. She tried to keep proper phone etiquette because she was more than tipsy from the wine.

"Ok great. Send me your address. And Kairo, call me Michael," he said.

"Sure, whatever you want!" Kairo replied sending him a text with her address before ending the call.

5555 Chrysler Dr. Detroit MI 48211

Kairo hurriedly got dressed. She dug through her closet to find something sexy to wear. Clothes were piling up as she tossed them into the 'no not that' pile. She wasn't in the mood to fuck, so she couldn't wear anything that screamed fuck me on the table please.

"Fuck, now I can't find shit!" she screamed having to dig in the pile of clothes she'd just thrown away. Before she knew it, 30 minutes had passed, and she still wasn't dressed.

Honk! Honk!

Michael got to her within 30 minutes, picking her up exactly at 8'clock on the dot. He was driving a classic candy red 2020 Lamborghini with black chromed wheels and all red leather interior.

"Shit! This will have to do," Kairo said sliding on a black Versace sun dress. It wasn't a dress for a dinner with a rich white man. As a matter of fact, nothing she owned in her closet screamed going on a date with a white man. Little did Kairo know, Michael was blacker on the inside than they come, just like Tommy Egin off *Power*.

He got out to escort Kairo safely to the car making sure she got in properly. Her neighbors were looking out their windows being nosy and gawking at this white man like they'd never seen one in the hood before.

"Wow you look absolutely stunning in that Versace sun dress." Michael complimented her as he pulled off smoothly into traffic getting onto I-75. Kairo flashed a warm smile at him and responded,

"Thank you. I did what I could in that 30 minutes I had. *Sniff! Sniff!* Kairo sniffed as she tried to name that familiar scent he was wearing. Is that Gucci Guilty?"

"Guilty as charged. You know your fragrances," Michael said impressed with Kairo nailing his cologne to the bone.

"My boyfriend, well he is my ex now, used to wear that all the time," Kairo said applying another coat of lip gloss onto her dry, cracked lips.

"Well that's unfortunate. He lost a beautiful valuable woman and now I'm here to keep that smile on your beautiful face," Michael said. His words were genuine, but his intentions were not. He wanted to be with Kairo, even if he had to lie to get her.

"I hope Andiamo's is good."

"Yes. I've never been there, plus I'm not picky."

"Good!" Michael turned up his jazz bumping to *Liquid Soul,* by Chris Standing.

Kairo was starting to spread her wings again after being in this damaging relationship with Delano. She still couldn't believe she really stabbed him. She didn't think she had it in her. Oh well, she wasn't about to waste any more time thinking about Delano while she was on this date.

The song switched to *After Hours,* by Ronny Jordan and she was impressed with Michael's music selection. She never knew that Jazz could be so relaxing, especially in this rainy weather. She bopped her head and snapped her fingers along to the beat. Michael glanced over at Kairo as he pulled up on the exit to 14 miles off I-75.

"You like that?" he asked.

"Yes, I do."

"Well then you will like this," he said turning on "Didn't Cha Know," by Joc Johnson. Kairo knew the beat as soon as it came on.

"Ahhh, this is 'Didn't Cha Know' by Erykah Badu but in a jazz style." Kairo was ecstatic.

"Yes, my lady. I also have something to show you once we get settled inside," Michael said as he pulled up for valet.

He got out the car, opened the door for Kairo, and they walked into Andiamo's together. The hostess greeted them at the door, gave them menus, and seated them at their table. Michael tipped the hostess and pulled out Kairo's chair. He was anxious to tell her the truth about her results, so after they sat down, he handed her a long yellow envelope.

"What is this?" she asked as she eagerly opened the yellow envelope. Her eyes widened reading her results. *Kairo Jenna Marie Taylor HIV status is NEGATIVE.*

"But I don't understand Michael. How is this possible?"

34

"Those are your true results," Michael confessed.

"I had to be honest with you. I didn't think you would ever date me because of my skin tone." Michael reached his hand out across the table and Kairo pulled back. She was now confused about what was taking place. She'd just gone on a killing spree a few hours ago only find out she was not HIV positive.

"Seriously? I'm not racist Michael. I will date outside my race. All you had to do was ask me. What a fucked-up way to have me thinking I was HIV positive!" Kairo snapped, now folding her arms across her body.

"I could have killed somebody today. Just take me home."

"I'm sorry. I really wanted to surprise you," Michael said, feeling bad for not telling her his real intentions. He watched as Kairo lost interest in him, pulling out her phone and texting or whatever it was she was doing while they were on their date.

"Please let me make it up to you."

"How do you take that back Michael? How?" Kairo shrugged her shoulders. She wished she'd driven her own vehicle because she was now very uncomfortable.

"Let me show you." Michael took Kairo's hand and left Andiamo's without ordering a single thing.

4

SAY YOU LOVE ME

*M*ichael took Kairo right up the street to the Oakland Mall. His plan didn't go as expected, so he had a plan B set in motion. He took her to this new upscale jewelry store called Unique Treasures that his sister, Michaela *"Mi-shay-la"* owned. Michael walked to the back to find his sister while Kairo sat up front.

She was relieved that she was not infected by that deadly virus, but that didn't mean Delano wasn't. Speaking of Delano, she gazed at her phone and realized he never called her. She looked in her blocked calls and he wasn't blocked. As soon as she began to dial the first three digits of his number, Michael returned with his sister, Michaela in tow.

"Hello! I'm Michaela, Michael's sister. Do you see anything you like?" Michaela asked introducing herself. Kairo looked around and saw diamonds on top of diamonds.

"Um, this is actually a lot to look at." Kairo said, still admiring all the diamonds that were 100% real. She couldn't make up her mind what she wanted so Michael suggested a beautiful diamond and gold bracelet from the Cartier Love collection. As Michael was trying it on

her wrist, Kairo glimpsed at the price tag, which read $40,100, and wanted to faint.

"You like it?" Michael asked?

"Yes, but don't you think this is pricey?" Kairo said. It wasn't like she wasn't used to this because she got expensive jewelry from Delano all the time.

"No, this doesn't even put a dent in my wallet." Michael laughed, handing his sister his credit card to charge.

"Well, you are very pretty and it's nice to meet you!" Michaela complimented Kairo as she

returned Michael's credit card to him. Kairo smiled back at Michaela before they exited the store.

"I'm really sorry to have you worry about your status. There is one more place I would like to show you," Michael said, opening Kairo's door to his Lamborghini. He put some more jazz favorites on as they drove to his penthouse in Southfield.

Michael was already wealthy. He didn't need to be a doctor to afford his way of living. His father owned a couple of hospitals and his mother was a big-time lawyer in New York City. Although Michael's parents were the bread winners in the family, Michael owned a couple of stocks in the New York Exchange and planned on partnering with Walmart to bring his home décor line on board.

"This is one beautiful view," Kairo said as she leaned over the glass balcony looking down over the entire city of Southfield. Michael's balcony had a 13ft pool and a warm jacuzzi on the other side of the pool. The string lights that normally decorates a Christmas tree, decorated the pool area and made the scenery a bit romantic. Jazz music played softly as Michael came out to join Kairo.

"Well thank you. I wanted to show you the view," Michael said bringing Kairo some White Moscato in a wine glass.

"What is it that you want? I'll give it to you right now." Michael glared deeply into Kairo's eyes.

Kairo was feeling the vibe Michael gave. She'd never hung out with anyone outside her race except Cali, but she was mixed. She hadn't felt safe in a long time, not to mention when she was with Delano, she still didn't feel safe.

"Is this your way of asking if I forgive you? Because I do." Kairo took a sip of her wine and Michael smiled at her.

"That is always good. Can I have this dance?" Michael asked extending his hand out to Kairo and taking her by her waist. They danced doing 1, 2 steps to *Ordinary People* by John Legend. He held Kairo tightly as they moved their bodies in sync to the music.

"You said you would give me anything." Kairo reminded Michael of his words and he nodded in agreement.

"Can you pretend to love me?" she asked, and on cue, Mint Condition's "U Send Me Swingin'" played through the speakers.

U send me swingin'

Oh u send me swingin'

JUST LIKE THAT he was speechless. Michael didn't have an answer. He leaned forward and kissed her on her soft lips. He didn't need to pretend; he always wanted to be with Kairo since he'd first laid eyes on her at work a year ago. He could see a life with her and that's why he chose to pursue her.

"Wow, I wasn't expecting that!" Kairo kissed Michael back, but her body was trembling because she'd never laid with anyone outside her race before. This was something new for Kairo to experience, and it was about to be one of the best experiences of her life with him.

Michael picked Kairo up and took her to his bedroom. He laid her down on his red satin silk sheets that hugged his king-sized pillow top mattress that he'd recently purchased from Beauty Rest. He planted soft kisses on Kairo's neck down to her collar bone, removing her dress with his teeth.

"Are you sure this is what you want?" Michael asked as he looked into Kairo's eyes.

She nodded, yes.

He gently caressed and sucked on Kairo's soft skin. She smelled like warm Vanilla and Honeysuckle, which was his favorite scent to smell on a woman. He began making a trail of wet kisses down to her breasts, sucking on both nipples gently. She arched her back while each nipple went in and out his mouth. His tongue danced ferociously around her areola's sending tiny tingles up Kairo's spine. He slowly moved down past her navel removing her pink cotton panties and exposing her beautiful shaved pussy that was shaped into a Mohawk. The sight of her well-shaven pussy and the sweet smell turned him on. He spread her legs wide and began to suck on her clit.

"Uuuuhhh," Kairo moaned loudly as she grinded on Michael's face. This was something new for him. He'd never had someone dance on his face before and he was amused at how delicately she moved her hips in a circular motion. Kairo gripped his head as he went further down licking her ass.

"Wait a minute!!!" Kairo screamed, but Michael kept going as he stroked his very hard penis.

"You ready for this?" Michael asked Kairo as he grabbed the golden wrapper out his nightstand. Kairo nodded even though she had no clue what Michael was working with. He strapped his condom on and entered Kairo.

"Oohhh, what the fuck!" Kairo yelled as she felt all of Michael's 11 inches inside her stomach. She wasn't expecting him to be blessed down there. She thought he was average.

"Michael, can you say you love me?"

"I love you," Michael said as he continued to make love to Kairo just as he always envisioned doing while they were at work. It didn't take long before they both reached an orgasm and fell sound asleep in each other's arms.

The next morning Kairo awoke to the sweet smell of maple hickory bacon. Michael walked into the room wearing nothing but a chef apron as Kairo was gathering her clothes off the floor.

"Oohhh Jesus!!" Kairo screamed, holding her clothes to her naked body. She was startled by Michael, not expecting to see him naked in an apron. He was scrambling eggs in a red skillet with oven mitts on.

"I'm sorry to startle you. If you don't mind, I cooked breakfast for you," Michael said.

"No, it's alright. What time is it?" Kairo asked searching for her phone. She had a shift starting at 11am and she still had to get home to shower.

"The time is 9:25am. Don't worry I already took care of your schedule for this week," Michael said leaving out the room exposing his pale white ass. Kairo sat in the bed with her hand on her head thinking.

"I know I didn't just sleep with my boss," Kairo said to herself unaware that she'd said it out loud and Michael was able to hear her.

"No, I'm not your boss, but HR doesn't have to know about this!" Michael yelled from the kitchen. Kairo slid her black Versace dress back on and joined Michael in the kitchen at his table. Once Michael completed cooking breakfast, he sat her plate in front of her. He'd cooked a big breakfast that consisted of cheesy scrambled eggs, maple hickory bacon, waffles, sausages links, grits and orange juice.

"Wow, I've never had a man cook for me before besides my old chef," Kairo said taking a sip of her orange juice. It was true; Delano never cooked. He was too busy running the streets so he would hire staff to do everything, including washing his clothes. She never had to do a single thing but live.

"You are so beautiful; did you know that?" Michael asked changing the subject but not on purpose. He was simply admiring her beauty. He couldn't believe she was there with him in his presence.

"Thanks. I really appreciate the breakfast, but I really need to get back to my place," Kairo mentioned so she could leave.

"Alright, let me get dressed. I'll grab my coat and I'll be right back," Michael said as he left the kitchen to get dressed. Kairo walked around looking at all of Michael's accomplishments he had on the brick wall and came across his Art Gala award.

"You never told me you were into art!" Kairo yelled to Michael.

"Yea, jazz and art are my thing," Michael replied as he entered the kitchen, fixing his collar on his navy-blue Armani Exchange bubble coat. Kairo turned around, bumping into his chest and dropping her phone.

"Whoops my bad," Kairo said picking her phone up and seeing that her screen was now badly cracked.

"Oh, shit!" she screamed.

"My bad. You need to get that fixed?" Michael asked taking the phone out her hands.

"Um, yea I can get it fixed soon," Kairo said as Michael handed her phone back to her.

"How about I take you to get a new phone?"

"No, I'll be fine. You have done enough," Kairo said referring to the $40,000 diamond and gold Cartier bracelet on her wrist.

"You sure? I can get you a new phone." Michael held the door open so they could leave. Once they got onto the elevator Kairo asked,

"Does it seem like I require too much for you?"

"No, you don't require anything. Just be a lady and I'll take care of you," Michael responded. He was the type of man that took care of his woman financially, sexually, emotionally etc. His mother raised him that way.

"Well that's good to know because we didn't even eat last night! Are we going on another date?" Kairo asked, following Michael to his 67' Camaro. This car was also Candy Apple Red, with tinted windows and black chrome rims. "Red must be your color."

"Yes to the date and yes red is my favorite color. What's yours?" Michael asked as he opened the passenger door to let Kairo in.

"Yellow. I like bright things."

"Well, that's wonderful. I'll keep that in mind," Michael said as he pulled off into traffic. "Do you listen to Hova?"

Kairo's face scrunched up. She was thrown off by that question.

"Yes."

"He is one of the dopest rappers alive from the BK," Michael said as "The Story of O.J." by JAY-Z blasted through his speakers. This didn't come as a surprise to Kairo, but she did think he only listened to country and jazz. She judged the man before he could show her who he was. Michael was raping along with the lyrics and sounded a bit like he was hood.

"You got a lot of hood in you suddenly. Where are you from? Kairo asked.

"I'm from Brooklyn New York, but I grew up in the Bronx since I was a teenager," Michael replied, taking Kairo's hand and kissing it.

"What about you?"

"Born and raised in Detroit. Did anyone tell you that you resemble Tommy Egan from *Power*?"

"No, but if that's who I remind you of, he's got to be one sexy ass man." Michael pulled up to Somerset Mall and parked.

"Let's get you a new phone."

It only took Kairo and Michael 30 minutes to go inside the Apple Store and come back out with her new phone. She had missed calls and text messages from Delano demanding to see her. She was surprised he wanted to see her after she'd tried to kill him yesterday.

Michael reached Kairo's destination, kissed her goodbye, and pulled off to go home. She smiled as she turned around and walked up her salty concrete stairs dialing Delano's phone. He didn't answer her call, but he answered her door instead.

"Who the fuck is that white nigga?" Delano yelled, snatching Kairo inside the condo. This caught her by surprise because she wasn't expecting him to be at her place. He had his arm that Kairo stabbed up in a sling. "There you go being a slut again!"

"A sluuutt!" Kairo yelled back at him. She couldn't believe Delano called her a slut.

"You heard me! You out here being a slut talking about me giving you HIV. How do I know you didn't give it to me?" Delano accused Kairo of cheating, but she hadn't had a chance to tell him that she tested negative.

"Don't judge my choices when you don't understand my reasons," Kairo responded. "I apologize for stabbing you. It turns out I'm not HIV positive after all."

"Excuse me? Wait a minute. Wait a fucking minute! So, you made me lose a million-dollar deal for my club and stabbed me in my shoulder to find out that you're not HIV positive?" Delano was in awe staring at Kairo as she moved so carelessly.

"I said I'm sorry!" Kairo screamed.

"Un fucking believable! You know what I'm glad we broke the fuck up because you ain't shit!" Delano shook his head and walked out slamming the door behind him.

Kairo was at a loss for words. She teared up and began to cry. Here was the man she was still in love with making their breakup official. Yesterday Kairo regretted her actions and wanted him to take her back. Just because she wasn't HIV positive didn't mean that he wasn't. He still needed to get tested.

SCUUUURRRTTTT BOOOOOOOM!!!! TRSSSSS!

Kairo looked up and watched as an 8,600-pound truck came crashing through her living room window. Glass and bricks were flying everywhere and Kairo had to run out the way because his truck came so far into her living room. The ceiling came crashing down onto Delano's front windshield puncturing through. She ran up to his truck that was now semi inside her living room and outside.

"DELANO!!!! DELANO!!" Kairo screamed as her nosy ass neighbors entered her apartment without her permission. That was the least of Kairo's worries. She pried open Delano's door with all her strength.

"Don't just fucking stand there! Help me get him out!" Kairo snapped at the neighbors who'd let themselves in.

When Kairo was finally able to get Delano out, he was inches away from the edge of the windshield glass. She checked his pulse, and there was none.

"Oh my god! He is not breathing!!" Kairo screamed as she performed CPR, but his body gave no response.

"Delano!!!!" Kairo screamed as the EMT came in to take him away.

5

UNTIL DEATH RIPS US APART

S plash!

"Wake your bitch ass up nigga!" Chino, one of Johnny's Sr. bodyguards said as he splashed a bucket of scolding hot water in Johnny's face, awaking him from a two-day coma.

"Ahhh!!" Johnny screamed in pain as the hot water touched his skin, burning him as it trickled down to his lap. There he sat in the basement of his own mansion tied up to a wooden chair. He sat there and thought about those innocent lives he'd taken sitting in a chair. Some he decapitated, some he made play Russian roulette, some he even drowned in pig shit followed by the gun, execution style.

Either way, he'd made some pretty fucked-up choices over the years while he controlled the drug trade from the four corners of North America. He was tough just a few months ago, but he was soft like a bitch now that his father was back. Johnny Sr. walked into the room smoking on his Colombian cigar.

"You're the fucking dumb ass of the year! How the fuck you lose 3 million dollars' worth of product?" Johnny Sr. said as he came closer to his son's face. He nearly died when he found out Delano set his entire

warehouse on fire with 3 million dollars' worth of cocaine and 200 of his employees inside.

"I did all I could do!" Johnny yelled defending himself, but his father wasn't trying to hear that.

"No, the fuck you didn't! You were probably so busy stuffing your mouth with dick. Yea, how long did you think your little secret was going to be a secret?" Johnny Sr. said. He was about to humiliate his son and make him regret he was ever born. He was left in charge once Johnny Sr. went upstate and put his business in a 3-million-dollar hole. Now he was about to rip 3 million out of his intestines.

"It's your fucking fault! You raped me and had other niggas touching me since I was four!!!" Johnny screamed unaware he was on the video camera.

"Hold up," Johnny Sr. said putting his hand up to signal the camera to stop rolling.

"You don't get to lie like you just did."

"You still that same ass lame motherfucka you were before you went away! It was me that called the cops on your bitch ass. I should have put a bullet in your skull when you were sleeping!" Johnny confessed. He was sick of his father's bullshit. The lies, the deceit; he just was over it.

Johnny Sr. didn't have anything else to say. He'd already heard what he needed to hear. This was the first time he'd heard of his son's betrayal and he wanted to kill him, but he wasn't going to just yet, not sitting tied to a chair.

"Release him. I'm done with him!" Johnny Sr. gave the order and confused Johnny. He'd just confessed to Johnny Sr. that he'd snitched on him and he was setting him free? He didn't ask any questions. He left without saying anything. He didn't mumble two words. To be honest, Johnny didn't know what to expect out of his father. All he knew was he'd better count his fucking days. Johnny was about to do

something he never would have done; ask Delano to take down his own father. Johnny could do it himself, but he didn't want to have his father's blood on his hands.

Two days later

Johnny awoke to loud fire truck sirens he heard rushing up his block in the middle of night. The time was 2am and he had beads of sweat dripping down his body, but he didn't have on the heat. His conscious was eating at him because of all the bad deeds he'd done while he was in charge. He could hear the piercing screams of little Chase's voice before he put a bullet in his head. This made him sick and sent him hurling over the toilet, waking TJ up from his light slumber.

"Love, are you alright?" TJ said as he ran cold water on a white rag before wiping Johnny's forehead and mouth.

"TJ, I did some pretty fucked-up shit, now I'm paying for it!" Johnny confessed before hurling up again.

"What hon'tee? I don't understand." TJ sat on the edge of the tub. He didn't give a damn what was going. He was falling in love with Johnny so quickly and rapidly even though they had just met almost a week ago.

"I need to be honest with you. Will you listen?" Johnny asked, finally gaining strength to get his head out the toilet bowl.

TJ nodded his head and replied,

"Yes."

"First, I want to apologize. I should have told you my status before we started fucking. I'm HIV positive," Johnny confessed, waiting on TJ's body language to tense up and read, *oh hell nawl, I better run,* but TJ just smiled.

"Oh, that's what's making you sweat and puke ya guts up? That's ok, because I am positive too," TJ revealed.

"That's partial—wait. What?" That fucked Johnny up. He wasn't expecting TJ to admit to his status.

"Oh, honey, being positive is nothing to be ashamed of. I'm going to love you regardless," TJ said, embracing Johnny. TJ already knew what came with this life because he was already infected.

"Ok, thanks for telling me. I don't think two positives can spread the virus, but there is something else I need to say."

"Well, what is it?"

"I need to make amends with Delano to help take my father out," Johnny said, getting up off the floor and walking back into the room.

"Well, what's stopping you?" TJ asked.

Johnny plopped down on the bed.

"I killed his four-year-old son while he was away!" he confessed.

TJ gasped holding his chest.

"WHAT!"

"Yea, I have done many things I'm not proud of." Johnny laid on his side face-to-face with TJ.

"We all have done something we're not proud of, but you can't let that get in the way of trying to do the right thing," TJ said, reaching his hand out to console Johnny.

"First thing you need to do in the morning is go pay him a visit."

"It's not gone be easy. I'm talking to a man that tried to kill me because I tried to take everything he ever had," Johnny sighed, turning on his back to face the ceiling.

"Baby, you gone have to put that pride shit aside and make things right. Can you do that?"

"I will try," Johnny replied nonchalantly.

"Unt, unt. If you had the energy to kill that little boy of his, use that same energy to make it right!" TJ said before turning his back on Johnny.

"You know what, you are right. I have nothing to worry about." Johnny grabbed TJ and kissed him. They spent the next hour making love before falling sleep.

ANNT! Annnt! Annnnt!

TJ's alarm clock went off, waking both he and Johnny at the same time. TJ searched around for his phone to hit the snooze button. If he could just get a few more minutes before he started his shift today, he would be straight, but Johnny wasn't having that. No man he was dating was going to be lazy.

"Here, don't be late again," Johnny said as he handed TJ his phone.

"I'm getting up, and don't you forget what we discussed." TJ got up, headed to the bathroom, and took a shower before heading to work.

Johnny stayed in the bed for an extra 30 minutes before he got up and got dressed. He was nervous. The last time he was in Delano's presence, he was smacking him with guns back at his mansion. He really wasn't sure how he was going to approach Delano and ask him for help, so he decided he would wait another day.

Ring! Ring!

Johnny's phone rang, and it was his dad calling wanting him to come outside. He went over to his safe, cracked the code, and pulled out his 9mm tucking it inside his pants. The last time his father wanted to meet, he walked into his own ambush that led to him being tortured. This time he was going to be prepared. His father could try to take him out the game, but he was going to pop him first. He was sorry it had to be this way, but it was until death ripped them a part in Johnny's eyes.

As soon as Johnny opened the door to his father's dark grey Lincoln MKZ, a thick cloud of white smoke escaped, choking him. Johnny's lungs were no longer used to the tobacco because he'd quit smoking a while ago. He didn't want to trigger any symptoms, nor did he want to speed up the AIDS process.

"Son, I want to apologize. We got off to a rough start. I think your sister's mysterious disappearance got me tight," Johnny Sr. said as he puffed on his Cuban cigar.

"I'm letting you have your space back."

Johnny sucked his teeth.

"How do I know you're not bullshitting me?"

"Son, I know you don't trust me, and I wouldn't blame you, but I do want to improve our relationship," Johnny Sr. replied handing Johnny's house keys back. He politely took the keys and realized they weren't the same keys that belonged to his mansion. So, he decided to keep quiet about it.

Although his father's intentions weren't clear, he kept his eye on him. Johnny Sr. had something planned up his sleeve. Johnny had just confessed a couple days ago that he'd snitched on him sending him Upstate for over 15 years. He knew that nobody in Detroit snitched and got away with it, so he was certain his father was plotting something, he just wasn't sure when he was going to strike. It was then that Johnny made a clear decision to have Delano kill his father.

"You heard anything about Cali's whereabouts?" Johnny asked, changing the conversation to make things less awkward.

Johnny Sr. took a puff before exhaling the same thick cloud of smoke.

"No. Detroit police is still out on the search."

"Alright, thanks B." Johnny put the key from his father in his coat pocket and exited his car.

As he was walking back to his house, he noticed a suspicious silver Impala driving slowly up the street. He knew his father was up to something, he just didn't know what it was. Johnny hurried and ran to take cover behind his black Charger as they began to open fire.

POW! POW!! BLLLLAAAATTT BLAAAT!

Johnny Sr. had set up a drive by shooting as an attempt to kill his son for snitching on him, but little did he know this was a failed mission. Johnny ducked low removing his 9mm. from his waist and opened fire back shooting the driver in the head. The car crashed into a pole, heading south on Broad Street and Joy Rd.

He didn't even check to see if the other man was alive. He jumped in his Charger, with busted glass from the gun shots, and headed straight to The Black Stallion. Johnny knew this was something his father had orchestrated, that's why he lured him outside. Johnny Sr. had no intention of ever giving him back his mansion. All he wanted to do was remove Johnny out the way and he wasn't going to stop until Johnny paid for snitching. Within 30 minutes, Johnny arrived at his destination and parked his Charger across the street from The Black Stallion.

"Hold up! You're not welcomed here!" The security guard put his hand up to Johnny's chest, stopping him from entering the club.

Johnny withdrew his gun and pointed it at the man's face.

"Don't fucking touch me." Just that quick, Johnny forgot he was supposed to be making amends with Delano. He humbled himself and removed the gun from his face. The security guard just stood there, unafraid of being shot in the face.

"My bad. I'm here to speak to Delano."

"Yea, he ain't here. He's down at Receiving."

"I'ight." Johnny turned around and walked back to his car, dialing TJ on speed dial. Good thing TJ was working at Receiving that afternoon because he needed to find out where Delano was.

"What's up baby?" TJ answered seductively. He was excited to hear his man's voice. Since Johnny was still DL, he ignored the seduction TJ was trying to give.

"I need you to look up a name for me, Delano Harris and tell me his room number," Johnny requested. He knew he was jeopardizing TJ's job, but Johnny needed to find Delano ASAP.

"He is in room 205 on level 2. Let me know when you get here." TJ ended the call swiftly.

Johnny wasted no time pulling off. His wheels were spinning so fast in the sloshy snow, splashing on the people at the bus stop, but he didn't apologize to them because he needed to get the fuck out of dodge. As he drove to the hospital, he was thinking about how his father might try to come back and finish him tonight, so he had to relocate. It seemed like since he'd gotten shot and his father returning home, he'd had a wakeup call and was turning over a new leaf.

Why does my father hate me so much when it was, he that molested me? Johnny thought to himself as he parked in the employee lot using TJ's code. He got to Receiving within 15 minutes and went straight to Delano's room, making sure to shoot TJ a message that he was there.

Delano was in a coma, laid in the hospital bed hooked up to a life support machine.

"Damn B, what the fuck happened to you?" Johnny asked as he walked closer to Delano's bed.

He just laid there like he was dead, but he was unconscious struggling to breathe on his own. This accident almost killed him, but he wasn't trying to attempt suicide, he just wanted to blow off some anger. TJ walked into the room with a cup of ice water and gasped after finding out he knew the patient.

"I know him. He's the owner of that strip club over there on Eight Mile," TJ said as he took a sip from his cup.

"You know everybody don't you?" Johnny asked.

TJ shook his head and replied,

"No, not really. This is Detroit. Everybody knows somebody that knows somebody."

"Ok listen, I need your help. Do you still have your place?" Johnny asked.

"Yea, I still got it. What's going on?" TJ questioned.

Johnny walked closer to TJ and caressed his face staring at him in the eyes.

"My father is trying to kill me. I need to know if I can lay low at your place for a while."

"Yea, that's no problem. My place is your place," TJ responded excitedly.

"Thanks. I appreciate you being there. Everyone that I know has turned their backs against me. This is only temporarily until I get back on."

"Baby it ok. I got you," TJ replied as he leaned in and kissed Johnny on the lips before he returned to work.

"See you tonight."

"T'ight."

Johnny walked back to the foot of Delano's bed after watching TJ leave out of the room. He was unaware that Delano was still able to hear everything that was going on. Johnny broke down and cried.

"Man, I'm sorry for the shit I put you through. I just hope you pull through this and get well soon." Johnny was finally breaking down and being remorseful for all the pain he'd caused in Delano's life. Now the trigger was on him from his own flesh and blood. He was now the weak link between Delano and him.

I'M THE WIFE, SHE'S THE HOE

"*M*alachi, can you please not argue with me and get your butt inside the damn truck? We have to go visit your father today." Kairo called out to Malachi, but he ignored her. He was acting very rebellious towards her lately, not listening and being very disrespectful every little chance he got. Although she and Delano were no longer together, she still felt responsible for Malachi. After all, she did kill his mother, and Delano laid in a coma hanging on to life support. He was a minor still, and wasn't old enough to drive himself to school, so Kairo stepped up to take care of him. Malachi was dragging his feet because he had an attitude with Kairo. He personally blamed her for the cause of his father's actions.

Ring! Ring!

Kairo's phone rang as she pulled off. It was Michael calling and she accidently pressed the answer button instead of declining the call.

"Hey sugar tits. When you gone feed me that sweet black pussy again?" Michael asked unaware that he was on the loud Bluetooth speaker in the car. This added more fuel to the fire that Malachi was brewing and angered him instantly.

"Damn, my father not even in the fucking ground yet and you got motherfucka's already asking to eat your pussy?" Malachi angrily folded his arms across his chest looking out the window scrunching up his face.

This caught Kairo by surprise. She understood his frustration, but he'd been disrespecting her since she'd been back home with him and it was time, she put her foot in his ass. It was now or never.

"Hold on, let me call you right back." Kairo pulled her truck on the side of the road and politely ended the call with Michael before he could respond.

Kairo was not experienced with disciplining teenage boys, but she remembered how her mother handled her teenage brothers when she was younger. Every time they would try or even thought about being rebellious, their mother would snatch them up by the collar. Kairo opened the passenger side door grabbing Malachi up by his collar and yanking his skinny butt out the front seat. She gripped his jacket so tightly that he was gasping for air from choking.

"Ay, who the fuck you think you talking to like that? You gone stop being disrespectful! I didn't do nothing to your ungrateful ass!" Kairo snatched him out the truck completely and he pushed her off him, causing her to lose her balance and fall to the ground.

"Man, fuck you! You're not my momma! You don't tell me what the fuck to do!" Malachi screamed as he stormed off walking up the street. He was right, Kairo was not his mother, but she was the closest thing to a mother than anybody had ever been in his entire life.

THUMP!

"OUCH! What the fuck!" Malachi yelled, rubbing the back of his head. Kairo took her Timberland boot off and hit Malachi. He had her fucked up.

"Where the fuck you think you going?" Kairo asked, getting up off the ground to chase after him. "I'm not gone ask you again."

"Fuck you! It's your fault my father is in the hospi—" Before Malachi could finish his sentence, Kairo punched him dead in the chest, knocking the wind out his lungs.

"I said you gone stop disrespecting me! Now get yo' ass inside the truck! Now!!!" Kairo yelled. Malachi stopped trying to fight her and got inside the truck without mumbling another word.

"I don't know what the fuck has gotten into you these past couple of days, but you are not going to disrespect me young man!"

"My bad," Malachi mumbled with his feelings hurt. He never thought Kairo would have knocked him in the chest. She punched him so hard, he could still feel the after effect stinging in the middle by his heart.

"It's ok. I understand the frustration, but I need you to be there for your father regardless of what he and I go through," Kairo said, finally calming down from knocking Malachi off his high horse.

"I already lost my mother. I don't want to deal with losing my father too!"

"Your father will get through this. That doesn't give you the right to act an ass towards me or anybody else. Do you hear me?"

Malachi nodded his head yes and then asked her what had been on his mind for the last couple of days.

"Is my father going to die?"

"No baby, he is not." Kairo had convinced herself that Delano would be alright. She knew that question was going to surface soon, she just didn't know when.

To be honest, she wasn't sure if Delano was going to pull through this time. The Voodoo Queen sent up another elixir that would keep Delano in a coma for a couple of days. Giving him that elixir without performing the ritual was a major risk, and it was no guarantee that he would live.

56

Kairo just sighed as she sat in the parking garage, afraid to leave her truck. She kept feeling like something was wrong. She and Malachi finally got out and walked up to the elevators as the bad feeling she had was now in the pit of her stomach.

"Lord, please let him be ok!" Kairo mumbled to herself as she dashed off the elevator going straight to Delano's room.

Finally reaching his room with Malachi a few steps behind, Kairo walked in and saw Nikki kissing Delano on his forehead. Although they'd broken up, she didn't like the sight of Nikki's lips on any part of Delano.

"Get the fuck away from him!" Kairo warned Nikki in a stern voice.

Nikki wasn't expecting to see Kairo so suddenly, but she'd been plotting on taking her out since the first day they'd sent her up north to prison.

"Bitch, what!" Nikki ran up on Kairo trying to take her out by using a box cutter she pulled from her pocket. Kairo ducked as soon as she saw the knife in her hand. Both women began fighting again like old times on Seven Mile and Gratiot.

"HELP! THEY ARE FIGHTING!" Malachi yelled to the nurses and they came immediately, breaking the women apart.

"You a weak ass hoe for pressing charges!" Nikki was talking shit again while she was kicking and screaming, trying to escape the male nurse's grip.

"Ma'am, calm down or we're going to have to ask you to leave," the male nurse said to Nikki, getting her to calm down in the hallway.

Kairo was unbothered. She walked over to Delano's bedside, picking up the fresh flowers that Nikki had just brought and discarding them in the trash.

"Depressing ass flowers make me sick."

"Excuse me, are you his wife?" the head nurse came in asking.

"I am!" both women answered at once, and Kairo cut the evil eye at Nikki.

"Bitch, she wasn't even talking to you! I'm his fiancée," Kairo snapped at Nikki and showed her ring to the head nurse.

"I'm the wife, she's the hoe."

"It's says here on his medical emergency contact, Nicole Turner. Is that you?" the nurse questioned, making Kairo look stupid. Delano never updated his emergency contact since he'd broken things off with Nikki.

"Ha, bitch!" Nikki said, griming Kairo up and down.

The nurse spoke.

"Ma'am, it seems as if his insurance is no longer available to keep his life support machine going. I'm giving you the option to pay $20,000, either in the form of a credit card or check; otherwise, we have to pull the plug."

Nikki was stuck. She'd just gotten out of prison a day ago and she had not a damn dime to her name. She swallowed her saliva as she looked back at those who were looking at her to make the right decision.

"When is the money due?" Nikki asked the head nurse.

"Today, preferably within the next hour."

"Ok, well I don't have the money right at this moment," Nikki said, shrugging her shoulders. "I don't want to have to say this, but we have no choice but to pull the plug."

"NOOOOOOOOOO!!!" Malachi screamed.

"Girl, you ain't shit!!! I got it!" Kairo said as she took her checkbook out and wrote a check for $20,000 that she was pulling from her savings. She couldn't even blame Nikki for saying to pull the plug. That was the type of bitch she was. As soon as Kairo was about to

hand the nurse the check, Delano woke up, snatching the oxygen off his face.

Everyone rushed over to his bedside. He had blurred vision and was unable to see who was in the room with him, so he squinted his eyes to adjust his vision so he could see. He could hear voices but was unable to distinguish who was who. Kairo reached out touching the shoulder on the side she'd stabbed him in. This made Delano have a flashback to when she first stabbed him and he grabbed her hand tightly, pulling her closer.

"Bitch, don't touch me!" Delano whispered to her before pushing her off him.

Kairo was shocked. Delano had never called her that before, so she stepped back as she massaged her hand while someone else welcomed him. Nikki approached him next. She touched his arm and he suddenly remembered their son, Chase, was killed. This made Kairo jealous, upset and angry.

"Oh, hell no! This bitch was about to pull the plug on you and you're hugging her broke ass first!" Kairo said with her hands twirling around in the air.

"Can everyone leave except Kairo please?" Delano demanded.

"Sir, we need to take your vitals," the head nurse said as she took his blood pressure.

"Fine, but I need to talk to her, so can you come back?" Delano asked. He was irritated by the nurse's response, so he got out the bed himself, pushed her out the room and closed the door behind him. Kairo wasted no time expressing her feelings.

"Well, what the fuck has gotten into you?" she asked. This was a different man she was seeing in front of her. The old Delano had never called her bitch, nor had he ever been so rude.

"Kairo, you got me fucked up! You think the world revolves around you and your bullshit? Where were you when I needed you? I had your back every fucking step of the way, but you have not considered my feelings at all. Not once have you appreciated me this whole time, but I'm not gone trip!" Delano finally spoke out on what had been on his mind, but he was careful not to say too much because he was still in love with her.

"I'm sorry Delano! I really am!" Kairo said as tears began to roll down her face. She knew she had been wrong, being inconsiderate about his feelings. "Baby, can I make it right?" Kairo touched Delano on his back and he had another flashback watching her being intimate with Jimenez.

"Get the fuck off me Kairo!" Delano said as he pulled away from her.

"You said it was over, right?"

"What?"

"The day you stabbed me in my shoulder and took your engagement ring off, you left me there to fucking die. You went to go get tested for HIV without me. You can excuse yourself out the hospital." Delano spoke calmly, but he meant every word that came from his mouth.

That was it. This was the craziest thing to break up over. Kairo had heard enough. She gained the courage to walk away from this toxic relationship. She didn't mumble another word. Instead, she wiped the tears away and left out the room, walking past, but not saying anything to, Malachi.

"Hold up Kairo! Where are you going?" Malachi asked as he chased after her.

She anxiously waited for the elevator. She kept pressing the button, but the elevator wouldn't come as fast as she needed it to. She was trying to escape the humiliation and not let Malachi or Nikki see her cry.

"Shit, this elevator is not coming fast enough for me!" Kairo said as she fidgeted through her purse to find her sunglasses.

Malachi finally caught up to her. "Why are you leaving?"

"Malachi, I got to go. I got to leave! Goodbye son," Kairo said as she turned to walk down the stairs instead of waiting on that slow ass elevator that finally decided to show up once she walked away. She sprinted to her truck and burst into tears as she played "Gotta Go, Gotta Leave (Tired)" by Vivian Green.

After she was done crying and being in her feelings, she needed to blow some of that steam off, so she did something she had never done before. She popped up over to someone's house unannounced. Kairo drove to Michael's penthouse doing over 100 mph on 96 to Southfield Freeway. As soon as she got outside his place, she called him.

"Hello?" Michael answered

"Hey, what are you doing?" Kairo asked, pushing her boobs up to look appeasing.

"I'm just relaxing and having a drink with a friend of mine."

"Oh ok, do you mind if I join?" Kairo asked, not giving a damn about who was there.

"Uh, I'm not sure," Michael said uncertainly. The woman wasn't just any kind of company. She was an escort that he was casually having sex with until Kairo fucked him again.

"Open the door!" Kairo demanded. Michael opened the door with his phone in one hand and his drink in the other.

"What Kairo? You can't just be popping up—"

"Just shut up and kiss me!" Kairo said as she sloppily kissed Michael, pushing him up against the wall. The woman Michael had as company was standing there in her sexy red lingerie watching Kairo kiss those same lips she was just kissing.

7

GIRL GIMME DAT-WEBBIE

"*A*hem, ahem." The woman cleared her throat to acknowledge that she was also there in the room with them. Kairo stopped kissing Michael viciously and looked at the woman standing there in her two-piece, red, lacy lingerie. She was an average height, brown-skin woman standing at 5'4 with brown, chinky eyes, a small waist, and thick thighs.

"Oh, did I interrupt something here?" Kairo asked, looking back and forth between the woman and Michael.

"No. Actually, Lulu was just leaving," Michael said, nodding his head towards the door giving her the signal to leave.

Lulu didn't make a sound, nor did she talk back, because she already knew what time it was. She just turned around and grabbed her things so she could bounce, but Kairo held her hand out and stopped her from leaving.

"No Lulu, why don't you stay? You eat pussy?" Kairo asked unexpectedly. She had never been with a woman before. This would be her first girl-on-girl experience and she wanted something to mask the pain she was feeling from the breakup. Kairo sauntered her way over to Lulu,

walking her fingers across her soft shoulders and around her back while admiring the sexy dragon tattoo that ran from the nape of her neck on down.

"If that's what you would like," Lulu responded, pushing her silky, long, curly hair behind her ears.

"Then you wouldn't mind if I did this." Kairo began to lick and kiss around Lulu's neck while massaging her breasts through her bra. Lulu enjoyed the feeling and rested her neck on Kairo's shoulder, swaying her hips back and forth allowing her to continue to gently massage her erect, pierced nipples.

"Damn, that feels so good!" Lulu moaned, turning around to kiss Kairo on her soft lips as she pulled her closer and rubbed her up and down.

"What in the hell did I just get myself into?" Michael questioned himself, shocked to see Kairo in action with another woman. Now aroused watching both women rub and kiss on each other, he finally shut the door, putting his Remy Martin down and pulled out his secret stash of cocaine. Sitting on the couch, he picked up a credit card and poured the cocaine onto the glass coffee table before dividing it into two lines.

"What is that?" Kairo questioned coming to sit down next to him and Lulu. She already knew it was a drug, she was just unaware of which drug it was.

"Ah, this is the Devil's candy. You want some?" Michael offered, but Kairo politely declined. She just watched as Michael divided a line for Lulu to snort.

Michael then turned on "Soulful Moaning," by Shawn Harris and slowly began to remove Lulu's red thongs with his teeth. Giving her eye contact, he licked slowly on her clit while Kairo sucked on her breasts teasing the pierced nipples with her tongue.

"Mmmm," Michael moaned, twirling his fat tongue around and sucking Lulu's freshly shaven pussy. He got so into licking Lulu's

pussy, he got aggressive with it, making Lulu moan and slow grind her hips on his face.

Kairo unzipped her jeans, removed them and played with herself while watching Michael eat Lulu's pussy to a satisfying orgasm. Being sure not to leave Kairo out, he leaned over to kiss her thighs before burying his tongue deep inside her vagina. She also danced on his face, holding his head in place as he took his face for a ride.

"Come suck this dick whore," Michael instructed Lulu. Then she got up and positioned herself laying down flat on her back as she sloppily sucked on him.

"Mmmm!" Michael moaned as he enjoyed traveling back and forth between Kairo's vagina and anus. He fingered her pussy and made Kairo beg for the dick.

"Please Daddy, give me that dick," she moaned, holding her breasts in her hands looking down at Michael eat her pussy like he was on Pornhub. He was showing out, spitting, slapping and playing zig zag with her clit. Kairo's knees began shaking uncontrollably as she creamed all in Michael's mouth.

"You know what? Let's take this to the bed," Michael suggested getting up and leading the way to the bedroom as they followed.

Kairo and Lulu were kissing and rubbing on each other while Michael stood at the foot of the bed massaging himself. He certainly was not expecting Kairo to be interested in women, but this was something that made him even more interested in her. He walked over to Kairo pressing his rock-hard cock against her ass while holding her breasts in place for Lulu to suck and lick on each one.

"Bend that ass over," Michael commanded, smacking Kairo's ass before lathering her ass crack up with his own saliva. Lulu laid back and enjoyed Kairo's warm tongue licking her passionately. Although Kairo had no experience eating pussy before, she ate Lulu like she was a fucking pro.

"OHHHH, MYY GOODD!" Kairo cried, as her knees began to get weak from Michael's tongue swirling around in her anus smacking both of her ass cheeks. He really got a kick out of eating Kairo's ass because he was already pre-ejaculating. Lulu scooted down towards Kairo's breasts sucking them as Michael entered Kairo's pussy raw. She threw her ass back on him, each thrust stronger than the other.

"Damn girl, you got some good ass pusssssyyy!" Michael stammered, trying not to cum so fast. He didn't want to look like he couldn't hang, so he quickly changed positions for both women to receive pleasure at once.

"Ride my cock and my face," Michael said, laying back on the bed as Kairo straddled him, grinding her hips in a circular motion and Lulu rode his face.

"Smack me and call me a filthy motherfucka!" Lula did exactly as she was told and was coming near a great orgasm.

Kairo arched her back as her body went numb, for she too was also reaching her peak.

"I'm cumming! Oh shit, I'm cumming!" Kairo's clit became sensitive. Soon after, this indescribable feeling ran throughout her body. Both Kairo and Lulu had mind-blowing orgasms at the same time.

"Fuck, I'm about to explode!" Michael screamed as he firmly held Kairo's body in place so she couldn't move. He was now deep inside her warm, tight pussy pounding her with all his might.

"Ahhhhhhh," Michael released, filling up her tight pussy with his entire army of soldiers.

Kairo looked over at Lulu who was looking suspicious about something, but she couldn't figure out exactly what it was. Before any one was able to get out of bed, Lulu spoke.

"Alright, we've had our fun, now where's my cash?" Lulu held her hand out demanding payment from Michael.

"Chill. I just busted a fat ass nut. Can a man catch his breath first? Plus, you said you weren't charging me for the pussy tonight!" Michael ranted. It then dawned on him that Lulu would want to get paid for the threesome.

"Either you give me my money, or I blow your fucking head off!" Lulu said grabbing Michael's handgun off the nightstand and aiming it at him.

"Whoa Michael! You didn't tell me this bitch was crazy and a prostitute!" Kairo said jumping up from the bed. This offended Lulu because Kairo didn't know her from a can of paint and she was judging her.

"Bitch don't judge me! You don't know shit about me!" Lulu reacted, now aiming the gun towards Kairo.

"Kairo, don't say anything, ok? I got this!" Michael said trying to protect her, but Kairo wasn't trying to hear that. She was gone regret saying this later, but pride was her downfall destroying her inside out.

The whole time they were fucking and having fun sucking, Lulu had the bug recorder on underneath the bed. She'd had enough time to place it before Kairo even showed up to the penthouse. Johnny Sr. had his escorts take the recorder on each Johnny or Jane run to ensure their safety. He didn't want to lose his escort ring in Detroit like he did back in New York and San Diego.

"Girl listen, if you don't take that gun off me, it will not end greatly for you. Last time I had a gun aimed at me, the bitch didn't make it to see the next day and she was my best friend. As a matter of fact, she didn't make it a full 24 hours," Kairo said, warning Lulu unaware that she'd spoken out about Cali's death to one of Johnny Sr.'s escorts. However, Lulu didn't know who she was talking about because she didn't mention any names. To Johnny Sr., she didn't need to mention Cali's name. She was still missing, and it didn't take a rocket scientist to know it was Cali she was hinting about.

"Are you sure about that? Because all I got to do is make one sound and my pimp will send his bodyguards up," Lulu said walking closely up on Kairo. She had her finger on the trigger, ready to pull it back at any moment.

Seeing that Lulu was serious about pulling the trigger to shoot Kairo, Michael dug through his pockets and pulled out $250.

"Here, this is all—" Michael said turning around to hand Lulu the money, but she squeezed the trigger. Hearing a clicking noise, she pulled it again two more times, getting the same result. The clip was empty. Michael forgot to reload the gun. He was now happy he'd forgotten to reload the gun or Kairo wouldn't be alive right now.

Lulu froze and dropped the gun.

"Oh my god! I didn't mean to." She panicked because the gun wasn't loaded. Kairo just stood there in disbelief that this bitch would even try to shoot her.

"Here, take this and go!" Michael handed the money to Lulu and walked her out the front door of his penthouse. He was not expecting Lulu to flip the way she just did. Any other time their transaction was mutual, just a nut and go. Michael returned to his room to find Kairo standing in front of the large window staring at the moonlight that shined into the room.

"I don't know what the fuck you got going on, but I'm not feeling it," Kairo said with her arms folded across her chest. Michael decided not to respond and continued to pour himself a glass of brown liquor.

"What was that all about?" Kairo questioned. She demanded to know what had just happened.

"Baby, if I knew you were going to stop by, I would have been prepared. You decided to pop up and now this happened. It's not that big of a deal," Michael said nonchalantly sitting down on the edge of his bed.

This upset Kairo, so she turned around facing Michael.

"Really? I could have been shot and killed! But fuck all that!" Kairo threw her hands up.

"Kairo please, I have a banging headache. Can you just come here and lay with me?" Michael asked trying to avoid an argument before it got worse. Kairo understood it was really nothing worth arguing over, so she decided to drop the conversation and walked over to Michael and fell asleep on his chest.

Waking up at 4am, Michael had a morning wood, so he rolled over on top of Kairo making slow and steady strokes inside her. She woke up as he flickered his fingers across her nipples causing Kairo to squeeze her muscles on Michael's hard penis.

"Aaaaahhhhh fuck, that feels good," Michael groaned as his penis went in and out of Kairo's creamy pussy.

"Mmmhm, you like that Daddy?" Kairo asked seductively, now holding onto Michael's ass pushing him deeper inside her.

"Fuck yea! Come here!" Michael instructed as he switched from missionary to doggy style and plunged himself deep inside Kairo's tight vagina. She threw her ass back, grinding and riding to another orgasm.

"OOOHHHHHH shit! I'm cuming again!" Kairo screamed before Michael picked her up and put her naked back side against the large pane windows.

"Uh huh fuck! I'm about to cum! Shiiiiiiitttt!" Michael yelled as he pounded Kairo harder, grabbing her ass and making her squirt her warm juices on him, the window, and the floor. This sent Michael over the top. He put Kairo down before ejaculating on the ground.

"That shit was amazing! My cock is still hard!" Michael's heart was beating rapidly.

"Well, let's go for another round," Kairo suggested, and Michael didn't stop her. He was a horn ball and didn't mind going for another round because he had stamina for days. Kairo moved down and wrapped her lips around Michael's hard pole, slurping up and down on him like he was a popsicle.

Slurp! Slurp!

Kairo sucked and deep throated Michael's dick the way she used to do Delano's. She had no doubt in her mind that Delano was never, ever going to find someone else to suck his dick like her.

"Ahhh, suck this cock," Michael moaned, rolling his eyes to the back of his head while she took her sweet time slopping his hard rod. She licked around the base and licked around the scrotum sending chills up his spine.

"Put that pussy on me baby." Michael grabbed Kairo and she sat on his face. Kairo quickened her pace, swirling and twisting her hips until she had another orgasm, for the third time.

"Oh shit, I'm about to squirt! Ahhh fuck!" Kairo moaned, trying to move away from Michael's face but he forced her to stay in place. Kairo's warm juices squirted all down his face as he sucked her pussy dry, not allowing a single drop to escape his mouth.

"Oh, shit!" she moaned when her body trembled, cooling down from that enormous orgasm.

"Whew, that pussy good!" Michael yelled slapping Kairo on the ass so she could get up off him.

She rolled over, exhaling and staring up at the ceiling while tears trickled down the side of her face. She couldn't believe things were over between she and Delano. Yet here she was laying up in another man's bed instead of fighting for her relationship.

"What's wrong baby? Did you not like the sex?" Michael asked, seeing the tears falling from her eyes.

"No, I'm sorry, I can't do this!" Kairo said getting up looking around for her clothes.

Michael grabbed her arm.

"You can't do what?"

"I can't do this! I have to make things right with Delano." Kairo snatched her arm away, getting on the floor searching for her shoes.

"Who the fuck is Delano?"

Kairo realized Michael didn't know about Delano and ignored his question. She continued to search for her shoes before she came across the bug that was placed under the bed from Lulu.

"What the fuck is this?" Kairo held up the bug to Michael.

"I don't know, but what I want to know is who this Delano cat is?"

"I don't have time for this!" Kairo said, letting go of the recorder and getting up to go search the living room for her shoes.

"Kairo, talk to me please!" Michael begged. She'd just fucked the dog shit out of him and now she had the nerve to ignore him.

"Michael, I will call you later," Kairo said before she exited out the door.

"Kairo!" Michael called out but she kept walking ignoring his voice.

Kairo pressed the button for the elevator and she walked on immediately. She was ashamed of what she had done and could not erase the memories out of her head. The damage was already done, and it was nothing she could do to change it. This would stay on her mind until she made things right with Delano, so she was going to pay him a visit. She was so focused on making things right between Delano and her that she forgot her phone at Michael's place.

As soon as she stepped off the elevator into the lobby, wiping her face with her hands, she was approached with a gun pointed at the back of her head.

"You're going to keep walking and step inside the fucking black van," a deep voice Kairo did not recognize whispered in her ear.

Kairo froze in her steps and was unable to breathe because this triggered the memory of her last kidnapping experience. When Cali and Johnny abducted her, she was brutally raped and humiliated amongst other things. She would be damned if she would take another bullet in her leg or get kidnapped again, so she elbowed the man in his gut causing the gun to fire. *POW!*

8

NOW YOU NEED ME?

" I gave you all the love I got,

I gave you more than I could give,

I gave you love

I gave you all that I have inside

And you took my love

You took my love,"- No Ordinary Love Sade

DELANO SAT at the edge of the stage sipping on Hennessey, watching his favorite exotic dancer, Exxxclusive, dance seductively to "This Is No Ordinary Love," by Sade. After all the shit he and Kairo had been through, this was his way of coping from their split up; drinking and watching naked women dance across the stage. It was his club so he didn't have to pay none of those hoes any attention, but he did anyway.

Honestly, he couldn't believe after searching for Kairo so many years, she would try to kill him. This was all a misunderstanding. He couldn't

even explain that he never fucked Cali raw, but none of that mattered. She didn't even want to give him a chance, so he had to let her go.

"Hey boss, you have a Johnny requesting to come see you. Would you like for him to come?" one of Delano's guards at the club asked. Delano turned around thinking about why Johnny would come see him.

"Yea, let him in." Delano got up to retrieve his revolver. He wasn't about to be caught slipping. If Johnny was gone be on all bullshit, then so was he.

Johnny walked into the club admiring the scenery. He knew he was the cause for The Black Stallion closing for a month, but it was back up and running like it never closed. He'd truly had a change of heart. He walked into the club with no gun not looking to seek revenge, but to make amends. They were approaching a new year next month and he didn't want to leave 2019 with a sour taste in the air.

"Whoa, whoa I'm not here on no bullshit!" Johnny said as he surrendered with both hands in the air. Delano had his revolver pointed at Johnny's chest and he was gone kill him if he was coming to extract revenge.

"Then what the fuck you here for?" Delano asked.

"Believe me or not, I'm actually here to make amends with you." Johnny took his vest off and hung it around the black high-rise chair.

"You killed my son. How the fuck are we ever going to make amends?"

"You're right, but you also caused me to be in a 3-million-dollar debt with the Italians. If it wasn't for my father resuming the Kingpin of Detroit, I wouldn't even be standing here. But I'm here and we both share a common enemy," Johnny said putting one foot on the ledge of the high-rise chair.

"Oh yea? Who might that be?"

"My father."

Delano put his revolver down and decided to talk to Johnny after all.

"So now you need me?" Delano asked.

"Yea, before his ass burn Detroit into a damn ditch."

"How is it that you think I can help you kill your own father?" Delano looked puzzled. Johnny was asking him to murder his own flesh and blood. He could never be trusted in his eyes.

"I just know you could. I've had a change of heart and I'm actually trying to live right," Johnny said trying to show Delano he really was trying to change.

"Really? How nigga?"

"I'ma start going to church on Sunday's singing hallerleiluyah in the choir and shit." He was now trying to lighten the mood by sneaking a joke in.

"Hal-le-lujah nigga?" Delano said, unaware that he was just joking.

Johnny nodded his head and scratched the bottom of his chin.

"Yea, I was bullshitting on that though. So, what do you say man? We cool or not?"

"I'll think about it. Right now, I don't trust you." Delano gave Johnny a pat on his shoulders. He suddenly remembered the conversation he and another young man was having in his room. "Aye, were you in my room the other day?"

"Yea, I came to check on you."

"Who was that man you were talking to?" Delano asked Johnny.

"That was my friend."

Delano gave Johnny the *nigga I know you lying* eye.

74

"Well I'll talk to you later. Let me know when you've reached a decision," Johnny said trying to avoid the conversation and left the club.

Lately Delano had been noticing that he'd been having these wild ass flash backs every time someone touched him. This had never happened to him before, so he thought to reach out to his aunt, The Voodoo Queen, for answers. As soon as he picked up the phone to dial her number, Channel Four flashed across the flat screen above the bar *BREAKING NEWS*. This caught Delano's attention and he turned up the volume.

"Just moments ago, Coast guards discovered a body of a female in her mid- 20's in the Detroit River. Now this by far must be one of the most horrendous crimes to have occurred in 2020. This woman was discovered brutally mutilated beyond recognition. Police say there is not enough information to release to the public about this woman's identity, but they are working nonstop on this investigation to find out who she is. Please check on your loved ones and friends. From the East side of Detroit, this is Jenny Marcello with Action 4 news. Back to you Markos."

The news anchor gave Delano a sharp feeling in the pit of his stomach.

"Tasha, hold the fort down. I got to make a run!" he said to his staff.

"I'm going to look for Kairo." He got to his rental and tried to dial her number but got her voicemail. He tried two more times and got her voicemail again.

"Shit!" Delano said getting out the car and returning to the club.

"Damn, that was a quick run," Tasha said to Delano as he walked behind the bar.

"Yea, Kairo's not answering her phone."

"I thought you said y'all were done?" She was starting to develop feelings for her boss, but he wasn't interested in dating her.

"We are Tasha, but can you close the club down? I don't need nothing else happening while I'm in the streets," Delano said before leaving the club. He tried dialing Kairo again and this time someone answered, but it wasn't Kairo.

"Hello," Michael answered.

"Who the fuck is this?" Delano asked catching an attitude wondering why the fuck Kairo would let another nigga answer her phone.

"My name is Michael. Who is this?"

"Man, where the fuck is Kairo?" Delano was boiling with anger. He could tell he was still in love with her because there was no way in hell he should be getting upset because her new nigga answered the phone.

"If I knew, I would tell you. She left my place two days ago, storming to get out of here and left her phone in the cushion of my couch. She said she had to make it right with some guy name Delano," he said, unaware that it was Delano on the phone because Kairo had deleted his number.

"Two days ago?" Delano questioned.

"Yea, two days ago. I'm surprised she hasn't come back for her phone yet."

"You mind if I come get her phone? Our dad has been worried sick about her," Delano said being careful not to give away his identity to this man that he didn't know, but Michael was already hip. Kairo's brothers were all deceased.

"Yea sure. I'll meet you in the lobby of my penthouse. It's 5555 Southfield Lane," Michael said giving the address to Delano.

"Alright, bet."

Delano ended the call and put Michael's address in the GPS. He felt it a bit odd that Kairo would just leave her phone at a random dude's house. He was not stupid by far. He knew she had to be fucking him.

He didn't feel bad for watching naked bitches dance across the stage after all. If Kairo could move on within two days, so could he, but he wasn't going to be petty.

Thirty minutes later, Delano pulled up to the hotel in Southfield and walked into the lobby. He spotted a white man dressed in a navy-blue Polo jogging suit walking towards him, but it wasn't Michael, it was just a regular hotel guest. Delano continued to look around to see if he could see what direction this man was coming from but he got nothing, so he dialed Kairo's number again and he answered.

"Hello?"

"I'm here. Where are you?" Delano asked still scanning the room for him.

"Ah, I'm at the bar getting a drink. Do you care to join my friend?" Michael offered.

"Nigga hell nah," Delano said with an attitude remembering not to give away his identity.

"Alright G. I'll be out in a bit," Michael said disconnecting the call.

BY THIS TIME Michael was drunk. He had been drinking since noon. He got up from the bar and walked out into the lobby. He spotted Delano immediately because he was looking around for him. He suspected this man was not who he said he was just from the conversation over the phone.

"Hello, I'm Michael. What did you say your name was again?" Michael said holding his hand out to shake Delano's. Delano never told him his name to begin with; he just wanted to confirm that he was someone other than her brother.

"What's up boss? It's Chauncey," Delano replied shaking his hand.

Michael chuckled rubbing the bottom of his chin.

"Man cut the bullshit. What's your real name?"

This caught Delano by surprise. He assumed Michael was onto him, so he decided to go ahead and tell him the truth.

"Delano. Why you so pressed to know?" he admitted.

"Yea, I knew you was that cat! We're fucking the same woman," Michael said handing over Kairo's phone.

"What you mean by that? You meant the woman you're fucking because this not that type of party."

"Just how it sounds, partna," Michael said, stepping up in Delano's face, griming him up and down.

"What the hell is wrong with you white boy? You trying to get your ass beat in front of all these people? Because I feel threatened."

"You should ask your bitch!" Michael said, taking his two fingers and pointing them in Delano's face.

"What the fuck you just call her?"

"A bitch. You lucky I didn't call her a h—"

Delano punched Michael in the mouth, busting his lip before he could complete his sentence. Michael was furious and began to fight back. Both men were thumping and throwing blows until the hotel security came to break them apart.

Michael spit the blood out his mouth and wiped the corners. He was astounded that he'd just fought this man over a woman. He really didn't mean to call Kairo a bitch. He knew that would be enough to set Delano off.

"Get the fuck off me!" Delano shook the security off him.

"Yea, you pussy. I hope I never run into you again because I'm going to kill you!"

Delano cut Michael the evil eye and proceeded to walk out the hotel. He wasn't about to go back and forth with Michael. He was a grown ass man. Besides, he'd already got what he came for, which was Kairo's phone. Now that he had her phone in his possession, this confirmed something had to really happen to her. He dialed Kairo's sister, Asia to see if she'd heard from Kairo, but her phone also went to voicemail. *What the fuck is going on? This is not like her to go without her phone. I wonder if Johnny Sr. has something to do with this. It's only one way to find out,* Delano thought to himself before he called Johnny.

"Wassup D?" Johnny answered.

"You said you need my help with something. Well, I need your help with something as well."

"Alright. What's that?" Johnny asked,

"Meet me at Somerset in a few. I got to pick up my son first and then I'll see you," Delano said before ending the call.

Delano scooped Malachi up from school and headed straight to Somerset Mall, where he met Johnny at Chick-Fil-A. He was really interested in what Johnny knew about Cali's disappearance. If he knew the body that was recovered earlier in the Detroit River was hers, then this could help him figure out if Johnny Sr. had set up a hit on Kairo like he'd suspected from the beginning.

"What's up man?" Johnny greeted Delano, but he just stood there not smiling or dabbing him back.

"Why the fuck are you talking to this loser?" Malachi complained remembering him from the mansion a while back.

"Chill out. Stay in yo' place. Here, go shopping or something," Delano said giving Malachi his credit card and he eagerly snatched it out of his hands.

"Wow! He got your ways already."

"Nah, I think he takes more after Cali. Speaking of Cali, have you heard anything else about her disappearance?"

"Nope. Her case is still open."

"Damn, how long has it been now?"

"Shid, past a month now. So, what's up? What you wanted to meet here for?"

"I need to know why you want me to kill your father. Why can't you kill him yourself?"

"I don't want his blood on my hands!" Johnny threw both of his hands up in the air.

"Nigga, but you'd rather kill my four-year-old son?" Delano was now getting heated thinking about Chase.

"Alright, alright. You're right. I can kill him myself, but I just asked you to do it. Shit, well you know Detroit's drug market has been on the up rise. My father came back trying to kill me for the cartels since I snitched on him, landing him 15 years upstate."

"If I'm not mistaken, you were once that ruthless drug dealer as well, so why are you afraid of competition? I don't want to be involved in your family affairs."

"But I've been on the run since my father tried to kill me and I really need your help. I have no more loyal men in my army. All have turned against me to serve my father," Johnny said as he begged for Delano's help.

"Like I said, I really don't want to get involved. You do what you got to do." Delano got up from his seat to go find Malachi. That little chat didn't reveal anything about Kairo being abducted, so he ended the conversation leaving Johnny to figure out his own plans.

Later, while Delano was on the way home, he received a call from Exxxclusive, his favorite stripper, asking was he in need of her services

tonight. It was 7 pm and it was around the time Delano would have her dance for him privately on the stage. He wanted to do things differently tonight, so he invited her to his new home. He decided he'd had too many memories in the house that he and Kairo used to share, so he moved from New Baltimore back to the city in the Boston Edison District.

Exxxclusive pulled up at the same time as Delano and he led her straight into the house.

"Why don't you get comfortable. What's your real name?" Delano asked.

"Gia," she replied.

"Yea, get undressed in here and I'll meet you here in a second," he said leaving her in his office he had in the family room.

Gia looked around the room, observing his house. She was really intrigued by the old antique house's look. The ceilings were oval shaped, followed by wood trim throughout the entire house. The freshly painted walls were dull and painted an off white color.

She continued to snoop around to see where she could hide her secret cam. She finally came across a photo with Kairo in it. She spit on the picture before wiping it with her ass and then returning it and placing the small camera next to it. Gia despised Kairo because Delano was a very handsome man and all she had to do was love him. Well tonight was going to be her chance to show him how much she wanted him, but Gia had a secret; a dark secret that she hoped he was willing to accept.

Delano knocked on the door twice before coming into the room and looking at Gia.

"I thought I said you could undress in here?" he said as he was lighting candles to set the mood.

"Yes, but you see there is nothing under this trench coat. I remove it, but it will defeat the purpose of my plan for you," Gia said seductively walking over to her music box. Gia seductively swayed her hips to the music while grabbing a chair as her prompt.

The mood is set,

So, you already know what's next

TV on blast,

Turn it down,

Turn it down

Don't want it to clash,

With my body screaming now

I know you hearin' it,

You got me moaning now

I got a secret set I wanna show you, oh

GIA DANCED TO "SKIN" by Rihanna while Delano dimmed the lights in the room. He sat down watching Gia's petite body glide across the chair. She gave him eye contact as she slowly began to remove her trench coat, loosening the buttons one by one, revealing her laced bra and panties. Gia's breasts were small like she was a child, and her skin tone resembled Kelly Rowland from Destiny's child. Her long 26-inch honey blonde weave flowed with her every move.

Delano took a sip of his Hennessy and watched as Gia made her first move, whispering sweet nothings in his ear.

"How do you like it Daddy?" She ran her fingers over his chest before sucking on his earlobe.

"Do whatever you want to do," Delano said giving Gia permission to have her way with him. She had a few things in mind. First, she wanted to suck on his neck and dry hump him until his dick got hard. Positioning herself onto his lap, she rocked back and forth until she felt his dick rise.

"Let me show you what my mouth can do," Gia said, unbuckling his pants and pulling out all of Delano's 8 inches. Gia didn't waste any time swallowing Delano's dick making it disappear down her throat.

Damn she swallows my dick like Kairo! Delano thought to himself while Gia did the head mop 3000 blaster on his ass. She went crazy gobbling on his nuts like she was a fucking turkey. Each time Delano's dick touched the back of her throat she would gag, spit, and use both hands. Delano's dick was rock hard, pulsating while inside her mouth.

"Fuck girl!" Delano groaned. It had been a long time since he'd had head this good.

"SLURP! SLURP!"

"You like that?" Gia asked giving him eye contact.

He nodded. Gia had this man weak to his knees, unable to breathe. Kairo might have sucked the breath out of him, but Gia sucked the soul out of him.

"Shit, girl don't make me cum!" Delano groaned, rolling his eyes to the back of his head. His mouth flew open as he enjoyed every bit of slob that ran down the shaft of his dick down to his balls.

"Take them fucking panties off," Delano demanded.

"Ok. It's something I need to tell you first," Gia admitted, kind of scared of telling her secret.

"What is it?" Delano asked.

The music changed to *Trading Places*, by Usher and this motivated Gia a little more. She had a secret and wasn't sure how Delano was going

to react to it, so she got up off her knees and laid back on Delano's desk.

"Can you remove my panties?" Gia said, dismissing the secret she was going to tell.

"Ok," Delano said smiling from ear to ear. He was finally about to get some pussy, so he got up from the chair and walked over to Gia. As soon as Delano attempted to remove Gia's panties, she closed her legs.

"I'm sorry. I can't do this! I was born a man."

9

WHAT HAPPENED TO KAIRO?

*wo days prior*

POW!

The sound of the gun went off in the lobby causing the guests to scream and scatter around like wild chickens. The gunman missed Kairo, grazing her shoulder and shot himself instead. She had no idea Johnny Sr. had sent his men after her. All she knew was she had to get the fuck out of their view. She bolted out the hotel, forgetting her phone at Michael's place.

"Fuck that phone," Kairo said out loud as she continued to run until she reached her truck. She was damned if she had to go through another kidnapping experience again. She ducked low as she struggled to get inside her truck.

SCCUUURRRTTT!

The sound of the black car screeched it's wheels on to the pavement of the concrete. They were looking for her and was damn near on her head. She wasn't about to stick around and wait for them to catch her, so she reversed her truck back so fast she hit a park car coming out.

Pretty soon, her abductors gained a sense of what vehicle she was in and this led them on a high-speed chase.

This way she knew she would lose them for sure, but they were just as brave as her.

Kairo was on the wrong side of 96, drifting from lane to lane and avoiding head on collisions with the oncoming traffic. Cars were honking their horns because she was doing the most idiotic thing ever driving on the wrong side of the freeway. Finally, having enough of swerving from lane to lane, she came up and drove down Glendale Street before coming to Woodward. They were still on her tail, so she ran a red light and darted in the middle of Woodward, and before she knew it, another car hit her.

SCCCUUURT! BOOOM!

Kairo's truck did a 360 in the middle of Woodward in Highland Park. The car collided into the front of Kairos' Range Rover, causing the front of her truck to cave in, but she only suffered from a piece of windshield glass in her forehead and a dislocated ankle.

"Ahhh shit!" she screamed as blood began to trickle down her face once she removed the small piece of glass that was lodged into her forehead. She touched her head again and saw the blood on her fingertips.

"What the fuck!" she screamed trying to loosen her seatbelt.

People were now gathering in the middle of Woodward to see what was going on. This stopped traffic causing a jam all the way back unto Manchester St. Johnny Sr.'s men decided to pull back since it was a lot of commotion going on and didn't want to have any witnesses.

"Ma'am are you hurt?" The young man who hit her truck asked running over to check on her. He was an average height handsome, chocolate dark skin man wearing athletic clothes coming from the Planet Fitness on Eight Mile and Woodward.

"No, I can't fucking get out!!" she screamed, still trying to wiggle her way free.

"Let me help you." He reached around to get her out, but he too struggled getting her out and decided to finally call the authorities.

"I'm going to stay here with you until the police come."

"I'm sorry, someone is after me! I got to go!" Kairo said still trying to break free. Then she went into a panic mode, hyperventilating. The sounds of the ambulance sirens were nearby and making its way through traffic.

"Hey, don't worry I got you! Stay with me," the man said, holding onto her hand.

"Why are you being so nice to me?" Kairo asked. She didn't understand why he was being so nice to her. After all, the accident was her fault.

"Because I'm just a genuine person. Now I hope you have auto insurance because your truck is fucked up pretty bad," the man responded.

"Yea we need more good people in the world, but ahhh!" Kairo screamed as a sharp pain ran through her shoulder that she was clipped in. She touched her wound and noticed more blood was oozing out.

"Yea thanks, but what's a girl like you doing running a red light?"

"I'm running from someone."

"From who?"

The ambulance finally reached the scene and the paramedics rushed over to Kairo to examine her injuries. They were able to get her out the seat belt and found out her ankle was dislocated.

"Ouch fuck!" she screamed as they put her on the stretcher. She was rushed down to Residence Hospital immediately. She was still paranoid, but it was not like she could run anywhere because her ankle was dislocated.

"Please, please call the police! Someone is after me!" Kairo screamed, alerting the paramedics.

"Ma'am who is after you?" the Paramedic asked as they continued to patch her up.

"Some people driving in a black Impala!" she responded, but they thought she was delusional from the accident and didn't believe her. What they didn't know was she was telling the truth and that same black Impala was following behind them while they took her to Residence.

"Ok ma'am, we have reached our destination. We're going to pop your ankle back in place. You're going to experience a little pain."

Kairo nodded in agreement.

"On the count of three we're going to pop it back in place and roll you in a wheelchair inside admissions to avoid the swelling. 1...2...3 *CRACKKK!*

"Ouch motherfucking Mary!" Kairo screamed at the top of her lungs.

"Ma'am, you ok?" the paramedic asked.

"Mmmm, I'll be fine." She had her eyes closed while tears rolled down her face.

Since Kairo was unable to walk, they rolled her in a wheelchair into the emergency room where they admitted her. The hospital was so overcrowded she had to wait in the waiting room until they were able to give her a room that was cleared. One of the abductors, who goes by the street name Scar, walked into the hospital and shot the security guards upon entry with a silencer.

Bodies were now falling and people began to get hysterical, screaming and running all over the place. Kairo heard the screams as she sat in the waiting room and decided to peek her head out to see what was going on. She saw the same two men from earlier and pissed herself because she couldn't walk.

"Listen the fuck up!" The hallway got quiet.

"We're looking for a woman. No one else has to get hurt. All we want is her, now where is she?" Scar said with a photo of Kairo in his hand and the silencer in the other.

"Please sir, she is in there!" an elderly lady who had to be in her 80's said pointing towards the room Kairo was in.

"Good looking old ass snitch!" Scar said shooting the elderly woman right in her face killing her instantly. The people screamed and mourned for the elderly lady. She did live a long life, but she didn't have to die like that.

"You didn't have to kill that old lady like that!" someone yelled.

"Shut the fuck up or you will be next!"

Kairo's heart sped up as she looked around the room to find an escape.

"Shit!" Kairo said as she realized she had no options to run. So, she did what she thought was best, which was to throw herself to the ground to crawl, but it was too late. The abductors saw Kairo trying to escape and put their foot on her back stopping her from moving.

"Where the fuck you think you going?" Scar said as he pressed his shoe deeper into Kairo's back.

"Please. What do you want with me?" Kairo asked, unaware Johnny Sr. had just walked into the room puffing on a Colombian cigar.

"You mean what I want with you?"

Kairo wiggled trying to get free from Scar's foot that made her felt so uncomfortable.

"Why are you doing this?"

Johnny Sr. picked Kairo up by her weave that was glued onto her head and threw her in the wheelchair.

"I believe you know what happened to my daughter Kairo."

"Fuck you! I told you I don't know what happened," Kairo lied, forgetting about the bug that was planted in the room. She didn't know what it was that gave her away. He pulled out the recorder and played her confession that she'd made to Lulu earlier.

This angered Johnny Sr. so much that he took his cigar and put it out on her skin burning her cheeks and she screamed to the highest of her lung's capacity. She knew she was fucked.

"Bitch try me again! Take her out of here," he demanded.

She looked up to see who was pushing her and the man who had on a black skull cap pointed a gun straight in her face.

"Say something and I'll kill you right here in front of these people!" he mumbled as he rolled her out the hospital and into a white van.

"Sir please. I don't know who you think I'm talking about, but that was not Cali. I have other friends as well," Kairo begged, trying to claim her innocence, but that didn't work.

The abductors opened the doors to the van and a foul smell hit Kairo's nostrils. The smell of rotten flesh reeked as they loaded Kairo into the back of the van. Then she noticed a body that was wrapped in the same dining room curtains that once hung in her home. She regurgitated and tried to scream but the abductors muffled the sounds out by placing duct tape over her mouth.

Johnny Sr. straightened his suit as he returned to his silver Jaguar and lit up another cigar. "Let's head straight over to the Detroit River. I want her to feel the same pain my daughter felt when she killed her," Johnny Sr. said giving the order. He was more than confident that Kairo killed his daughter. He didn't need to prove shit. It was a reason Cali sent that text message before she disappeared and he was going to get to the bottom of it no matter who interfered.

After that long drive, they finally reached the Detroit River off Belle Isle. They took Kairo out and rolled her in front of four people. They

were all on their knees with their hands tied behind their backs and black sacks covering their faces.

"Why do you have these people here?" Kairo asked. She was confused as to why they had these people here with her.

"How much do you love your family?" Johnny Sr. asked, walking up to Kairo. He had Scar to record what was taking place.

"What kind of question is that?" She rolled her eyes unaware that the four people that was in front of her was her family.

"Remove their bags!" Johnny Sr. commanded.

Kairo's eyes widened as she watched each bag being removed, revealing each family member and she screamed so loud that the Canadian residents could hear.

"Please don't kill my father!! Please! Not my sisters!"

"Again, how much do you love your family?" Johnny Sr. asked, breathing in Kairo's face and yanking her weave.

"Ooouuchh! You son of a bitch!" she screamed from him pulling her hair, and Johnny Sr. nodded his head to one of the men with a gun in their hands.

POW!

The gunman shot one of Kairo's sisters in the legs. Her name was Natori, Kairo's third eldest sister. The words couldn't escape from Kairo's mouth fast enough before blood splattered over her face. Natori's muffled screams were silenced as the next bullet entered and exited out her brain. Kairo's heart felt like it was shattered into pieces. She grabbed her chest and fell onto the ground.

"Get your weak ass up! Again, how much do you love your family?" Johnny Sr. asked again. He was trying to make a point and it was valid. Nobody was going to get away with killing his flesh and blood. Kairo was going to pay.

"A lot, goddamn it! I love them a lot! Ok!" Kairo screamed, as she laid on the cold ground.

"You don't get to wail and cry now! You killed my fucking daughter!" he said, picking Kairo up off the ground.

"You were her best friend!"

"I didn't—"

"Don't fucking lie to me! I'll shoot the next motherfucka myself," Johnny Sr. said pointing the gun directly at Kairo's father. He purposely squeezed the trigger and shot him in his left thigh.

"Oops! My bad!" Johnny Sr. laughed.

"NOOOOOO!!" Kairo screamed.

"You don't love your family. You're sitting here letting them pay the price for your sins. Isn't that right Pastor Taylor?" Johnny Sr. asked Kairo's father who was now going into shock from the gun wound and the cold weather.

"What do you want me to do? It seems like your mind is already made up!" Kairo questioned.

"Confess and set your family free!" he said.

"Ok, ok, ok I killed her! I killed that bitch!" Kairo confessed.

"Ahhh that's all I wanted to know!" Johnny Sr. turned around shooting the remaining two sisters, Asia and Diamond to their deaths. He lied. He wasn't going to let anyone live.

"Dispose their bodies in the Detroit River," he demanded.

"WAIT! WAIT! WAIT!!! You said you would set them free! You lied to me!" Kairo yelled. She was now furious.

"Yes because you lied to me. Now watch as I decapitate your father!" Johnny Sr. said as he fired up the power saw and walked over to Kairo's father. *SSSSSZZZZZZZZZZZZZZ!!!*

10

???

*D*elano couldn't believe what he'd just heard. How could he have been so blind to the fact that this man was not a woman? It was easy for him to overlook because Gia was a transformed woman. Everything was completed with hormone shots. Her Adam's apple was shrunken and her hands and feet were smaller than most men. She just wasn't going to remove that tail that was tucked between her legs.

"MAANNN!!! What the fuck did you just say?" Delano asked. He needed to be clear that he did not just let a man seduce and suck on his dick.

"I said, I was b-b-born an m-m-man," Gia stammered, trying to get the words past her teeth and the truth through her lips. She was born as Geo Alexander but was dancing at The Stallion to make a living.

Delano laughed, running his hands down his face. He literally couldn't believe Gia would have the audacity to even try him like this.

"You know you're got to die tonight right?" Delano warned Gia that she was not going to see the sun rise.

"What do you mean? You don't know shit. Why would you kill me?" Gia said in her male voice offended by Delano's reaction and scooted down off the table. This was not the kind of reaction she was expecting. She thought Delano could tell she was man. He sure was eyeing her like a damn piece of candy.

"And I don't want to fucking know! Get the fuck out my house before I murk your ass!" Delano said, now getting agitated.

"But I'm a woman! See!" Gia said pulling her panties down. Her tail was tucked and not visible to see. Delano didn't even have to look because he wasn't going to. This made him so mad he tightened his fist and punched Gia in her mouth, making her gasp.

"You're fucking crazy!!!" Gia screamed. She immediately began to pack and ran out to her car.

"Oh, I'm crazy? I'm going to kill you! You better get the fuck on while you're ahead!"

Delano was so enraged with anger that he followed behind Gia without giving her the chance to get out of sight. She was not about to just get away with this gay shit she'd just pulled. He did say she had to die, and he meant it.

Once he caught up to Gia at the light on Grand Blvd and Rosa Parks, it was all over. Delano pulled up next to Gia's vehicle and smiled before squeezing the trigger. Glass shattered from the bullet penetrating the windows and exiting out through the other side. Gia's brains were spilled all over the windshield and the two front seats.

HONNNNNNNNNNNNNNK! The sound that the car horn made while her body was left slumped on the steering wheel for the Detroit Police to find. *SSSCUUURRRTTTT!!* Delano pulled off so fast with his tires burning skid marks in the street. He escaped without any witnesses to see what he'd done. He ran a few lights and bent a few corners to avoid any police that were out patrolling tonight. Although this had never

happened before, no man was gone live to see the next day if they'd ever violated him.

He immediately dismissed the thoughts that lingered in his head about Gia before finding out she was born a man and swung by Kairo's crib. He was starting to miss her and knew she wouldn't be home, but he still decided to go over there anyway.

Once he reached her place, it was desolate with blue renovation tarps covering the front of her house. He regretted running through her condo with his truck. This could cause her serious repercussions, such as her getting an eviction or being sued for property damages. He knew he had to get her back home with him where she belonged, so he went to the next place she would be, which was her sister, Asia's.

He drove to Grosse Pointe Woods where Asia resided, and her place was also desolate. The mail was piled up on the porch, the snow hadn't been shoveled, and her car was still in the driveway with no tire tracks. *Ok, this is a bit awkward. Maybe she is sleep,* he thought to himself. He walked on the porch, and knocked and knocked, but got no answer, nor detected movement from inside the house.

"Maybe they're all at their father's house," Delano said to himself.

He decided to check one more place, her father's home in the Indian Village. After all, it was around Christmas time, so the family could be together for the holidays. Delano got inside his car and drove to Indian Village. As he drove by, he noticed the side door to the house was wide open as if someone had broken into the home while no one was there.

"Alright, what the fuck is going on here?" He pulled up to Kairo's father's house. His home was also desolate, but there was something odd going on. So, he decided to go look and parked his car in the driveway behind Kairo's father's Benz truck. He grabbed his revolver from the glove compartment and slowly walked up to the side of the house.

It was completely dark and the only light that was visible was the moonlight that reflected off the snow through the night. The wind rustled through the tree branches, creating a howling noise as he crept in the dark finally approaching the side door. Once he stepped his foot inside the house, he covered his nose to avoid the foul stench of a dead corpse.

His stomach grew weak as he noticed the bloody trail of footprints and thinking about what he might see if he was to turn that corner. He flicked on the lights so he could see his way around to that awful smell that lingered throughout the house.

He followed the blood splatter along the tan walls before coming to the bathroom where he stopped, paused, and gathered his thoughts. Delano wasn't sure what he was going to see once he opened the door, but he had to prepare himself for whatever it was. He reached his hand out to slowly push the door open.

RING! RING!

Delano got a call from Nikki that interrupted him from pursuing what was behind the door. He didn't want to ignore her because he'd already put her through a lot and she still was grieving over their four-year-old son.

"Was sup Nikki?" Delano answered coolly. He was distracted by her call and agitated by the smell that was awfully foul.

"Hey you! I know it's late, but I was feeling alone and wanted to know if you wanted company," Nikki slyly asked. She wanted to lay on his chest and talk about memories of Chase.

"Yea meet me at the house in 15 minutes," Delano said and before Nikki could respond, he ended the call. Forgetting to hold his breath, he threw up from the smell. He needed to be sure that this wasn't Kairo or any of her family members.

"Alright, let me try this shit again," Delano said wiping the vomit from the corners of his mouth.

Finally, he kicked the door open and flies swarmed around the bath-room and the tub. Delano still had his nose covered and turned on the light. He swiftly pulled back the clear bloody curtain and found the headless body of Kairo's father lying upright in the tub with rigor mortis. There was a message attached to the middle of his chest and Delano snatched the card off.

"Eye for an eye, tooth for a tooth, family member for a family member. Kairo killed my daughter, now do you have a clue who?"

Delano balled the note up furiously. It was almost as if they knew he was going to be the one to find the body. He called the police and reported the gruesome discovery and didn't wait around for them to show up because it would literally take the police hours before they responded to a crime scene. Besides, he couldn't take the smell anymore.

This worried Delano. He needed to find Kairo immediately. Now that Johnny Sr. was aware of Cali's death, he feared the worst had happened to her, so he found himself calling Johnny to see what he knew as he headed home. The time was 1:02 am and Nikki was constantly blowing his phone up.

"Nikki, I said I'll be there in a minute!" Delano snapped into the phone irritated by her impatience.

"I've been waiting for you for over 30 mins now!"

"Alright, hold tight. Let me make this call real quick," Delano said before hanging up and dialing Johnny's cell.

Three rings and Johnny finally answered. "What's the deal?"

"Where the fuck is Kairo?" Delano asked. He assumed Johnny knew about Kairo's whereabouts.

"Nigga, how am I supposed to know? I'm in bed sleeping. The ques-tion is why are you calling me this early?" Johnny questioned because he was confused.

"I just found her father decapitated in his own tub with a note attached to his body in the form of some kind of riddle."

"That's definitely some kind of shit my father would do. I tell you what, meet me at the Eastland Food court tomorrow at 2PM. I'll be east all day."

"Alright bet. I'll see you soon," Delano said, ending the call and proceeded to walk into the house.

He didn't want to alarm Nikki. She was sound asleep comfortably in his bed, so he quietly walked past into the master bathroom to take a hot shower. He let the hot water run down on his skin while he fought the tears as he mourned Kairo's father. He wasn't getting any answers standing in there, so he tried not to worry about it. But he couldn't help but to worry, so he stepped out, wrapping his mint green towel around his waist, covering his penis and fixed him a quick drink.

"What's the matter? You can't sleep?" Nikki asked walking over to Delano and wrapping her warm arms around his wet torso.

"No, I seen some shit tonight. Maybe you can help relieve me from this stress," Delano said turning around to face Nikki. He stared in her soft brown eyes and lifted her chin to kiss her lips, but she hesitated.

"What's the matter?" Delano asked, holding her face in the palm of his hands.

"It's been so long since we've been intimate," Nikki responded feeling insecure about her body. Since she'd been in prison, she'd picked up a little weight. But none of that mattered to Delano. He needed some pussy and Nikki was the closest person.

"None of that matters. I still love you the way you are," Delano said reassuring Nikki and she immediately came out of her clothes. He kissed her lips and planted warm sloppy kisses along her neck. Nikki massaged his penis until it turned rock solid in her hand, before getting on her knees to suck on it. Flashbacks of Gia sucking his penis earlier that night crept in his mind and he got soft in Nikki's mouth.

"Uh, what just happened?" Nikki asked taking Delano's flaccid penis out her mouth. She hadn't the slightest idea as to what he'd seen tonight. Delano huffed and tried not to display any emotions.

"I can't explain it. Let's just go to sleep and try again in the morning," Delano said walking over to the bed. Nikki didn't even argue. This was the first time she'd ever listened without talking back. She climbed into bed and fell asleep on Delano's chest while he laid there wide awake thinking about Kairo before finally falling asleep at 4 am.

Ring! Ring!

Delano woke to the sound of his phone ringing nonstop as he looked at the screen and saw it was Tasha calling from The Black Stallion. He sat up in bed rubbing the sleep out his eyes before answering the call.

"Hello," Delano answered coolly trying to gain strength to wake up completely,

"Boss, you need to come down here immediately. Something happened to Exxxclusive last night," Tasha said in a panicking voice, unaware that she was talking to the one person who'd killed her.

Delano groaned as flashbacks of the murder ran across his mind.

"Give me a minute. I'll be there," he said hanging up the phone.

"Is everything alright?" Nikki asked waking and sitting up in bed.

"Yea. One of my dancers was murdered." He got up to retrieve some clothes out the closet. "Do you mind keeping an eye on my son for me?"

"Mmmhm, I think I'm going to need a few dollars to keep me from being bored," Nikki said looking at her nails. Delano just shook his head before throwing Nikki $500 in crispy hundreds.

"Alright, I got to go to the club really quick. Don't hesitate to call me if you need anything." He got dressed and headed over to the club. He wasted no time getting to The Stallion. He didn't want to make it

obvious that he didn't care. Everyone knew she was his favorite exotic dancer, so it would be odd if he didn't show up. As he was walking to the bar, he saw the staff had already built a memorial in honor of Exxxclusive aka Gia.

"AHHHHHH DELANO!" the shot girl screamed dropping the entire platter of customer drinks onto the floor.

Delano ran over to see what was going on and his eyes grew wide. He couldn't believe what he was seeing.

"Oh my god!" Delano yelled.

YOU SNOOZE, YOU LOSE

"Present day"

*W*HAMM!

"Bitch, wake your ass up!" Johnny Sr. said to Kairo as he tightly gripped the brass knuckles before punching her in her face. Kairo was in serious need of medical attention but Johnny Sr. wanted her to suffer first. She was badly beaten for two days straight, and her clothes reeked of piss and shit because they denied her of her bathroom rights.

Johnny Sr. had Kairo beaten until she begged for mercy, but she never said a mumbling word out of fear that she too might just die senselessly like her father and siblings. Now her entire immediately family had been killed by the hands of the enemies. The pain soared across Kairo's body as Johnny Sr. struck her in the face again.

"You deserve all this pain I'm giving to you!" Johnny Sr. said before punching Kairo in the face again, this time busting her lips. Her eyes

and face were so badly swollen with lumps and bumps that you would think she'd had an allergic reaction.

"Please just kill me already!" Kairo begged, finally having enough of being tortured. But Johnny Sr. had other plans for her.

"Not just yet. I know you couldn't have done all this by yourself. You had some help didn't you?" He was now in her face.

"I acted alone," Kairo lied. She was no snitch and she wasn't going to snitch either.

"LIAR!" he screamed in her face.

"I should break every fucking bone in your body!"

"Please just kill me already. You already killed my family. What more do you want from me?" Kairo said as the tears cascaded down her cheeks.

"You already know what I'm asking. That's on you if you want to keep taking the blows for Delano," Johnny Sr. said before standing in the corner lighting up a Colombia cigar. Kairo's skin was filled with cigarette burns and blisters; looking like a bad tattoo of infected Leopard spots.

"He has nothing to do with this!" Kairo mumbled.

"I refuse to believe a weak bitch like you killed my daughter all by yourself!"

"Trust me, if I wasn't in this chair I would kill you myself just like I killed Cali. Nothing about me is weak." Kairo spit the blood out her mouth. She couldn't let the smell of fear wave across Johnny Sr.'s nose. If he detected any kind of fear, he was going to use that to his advantage.

"Boss, the Detroit Police is here to speak with you about the body found in the Detroit River yesterday." One of Johnny Sr. guards came into the room and said to him.

"Interesting. I'll be right back. Put her back into the room," Johnny Sr. said as he left the room to attend to a small private matter.

Kairo sat still in the corner finally able to let out a deep exhale, catching a break from the torturing that Johnny Sr. was inflicting on her. She felt weak and silently wept in the room grieving for her family.

"God, I need you!!!" Kairo cried out on her knees with her face in her lap.

Knock knock!

A tall skinny man knocked on the door before entering in the cold dark room finding a very fragile Kairo on her knees in the far right corner.

"Hey, let's get you out of here before he kills you," he said as he quickly approached her. She was startled and pushed herself back up against the brick wall because she could barely see who he was. The room was dark and her eyes were swollen from two days of straight torture. "Don't be afraid. I only want to help you."

"Help me?" Kairo tried to look up at the young man.

"But you can get killed trying to help me."

"And that's a risk I'm willing to take. I think he is over doing it the way he is torturing you. I didn't sign up for this. You remind me of my own sister Capri. As a matter of fact, you resemble her; same complexion and everything. Do you think you could follow me this way? I know a way through the back to the car," he said looking out for any guards that may have been coming to check on their prisoner.

"Wait! I can't walk! My foot is not allowing me to stand!" Kairo said reaching her hand out to the man.

"Alright, I'm just going to have to carry you. On three, I'm going to lift you over my shoulders. 1....2....3!" The man lifted Kairo up and escaped through the backdoor. He placed her on the passenger side of

the car and took off. What he didn't know was that the car had a tracking device, so it wouldn't be long before they were found.

"Do you have a place in mind where we can go?" he asked.

"Yea." She paused, taking a deep inhale.

"Take me to The Black Stallion. You know where that is?" Kairo asked trying to adjust herself and get comfortable in the seat. She knew Delano would be there and he would help her whether they were together or not.

"Yes ma'am. I'm from the Eastside. I know exactly where it's located. I'm surprised you don't remember who I am," he said as he drove over the salty streets on the city's Eastside.

"No. I could barely see who you are," Kairo replied.

She was in a lot of pain, emotionally and physically. Her hands and arms where covered with blisters from the cigars Johnny Sr. put out on her skin, her face was swollen so badly with lumps from the brass knuckles he'd used across her face, and her eyes were black and purple with a busted blood vessel in both eyes. It was amazing she'd made it this far with a broken heart and a badly bruised body.

"Ok, well it doesn't matter. Let's get you somewhere safe," the young man said.

"Thank you for helping me escape. I really appreciate it!" Kairo rubbed around her throat and remembered the tight rope that was used to drag her around on Belle Isle.

"Yea no problem," he replied.

She still remembered her father's death like it was yesterday. It was no way she could ever forget. Watching his head being removed from his body with a power saw was disturbing. It was enough watching her sisters take the bullet one by one.

"So, did you really kill his daughter, California?" he asked Kairo interrupting her from her thoughts. He'd heard the rumors floating around and wanted to hear the truth for himself, straight from the horse's mouth.

"Yes, I did!" Kairo said proudly, not regretting a damn thing she'd done.

"Wow." He chuckled.

"I still remember when you killed my partner in front of me when you first got kidnapped," he admitted and this brought Kairo's memory back.

"Roy???" Kairo questioned to be sure it was him, and she was right.

"Ahhh, now you remember, right when we're pulling up to The Stallion," Roy Allen jokingly said in a sarcastic matter.

"Boy, stop playing and help me get inside please," Kairo insisted, swinging her full body to the side to get ready to walk into The Black Stallion. As soon as she got out the car, the security gasped at the sight of her. They knew who she was but was not used to seeing her mangled up like this. They stepped aside and opened the door for her as she limped inside. Kairo didn't care about who saw the shit stains on her pants or the dried blood from her nose. She'd already lost more than she ever had. As soon as Kairo turned into the club, she felt weary and collapsed onto the floor in front of the shot girl.

"AHHHHHH DELANO!" the shot girl screamed, dropping the entire platter of drinks crashing onto the floor.

Delano ran over to see what was going on and his eyes grew wide. He couldn't believe what he was seeing.

"Oh my god!" Delano yelled, and he ran to check her pulse.

"Kairo, what the fuck happened?"

"She was badly beaten and tortured," Roy said to Delano.

"I'm sorry, who are you?" Delano asked. He wasn't familiar with his face at all.

"My name is Roy Allen Jr. I used to work for Johnny, sir," he replied.

"Good to know Roy. Now help me get her in my car right now!" Delano demanded as he picked up a very fragile Kairo. She smelled foul, but he didn't care how she smelled as long she was alive, that's all that mattered to him.

"Thanks, bruh. I got it from here," Delano said slamming the car door.

"Alright, I'll catch up with you lat—" Roy Allen Jr. paused before looking down at the blood spot that was forming in the middle of his chest. The white tee was now soiled with blood as a couple more fatal shots pierced his body not exiting. Delano watched as Roy's body slowly hit the ground and he pulled off quickly. He grabbed his revolver out the glove compartment and started shooting shots striking two men.

SCCCUUUURTTTT!

Delano's wheels burned against the dry pavement as he sped up Eight Mile to get to 94. He saw the police sitting on the other side in Harper Woods but decided to speed right past them because Johnny Sr.'s men were after him, leading all three cars on a high-speed chase.

He approached 94, speeding down the ramp doing over 75 mph, avoiding a collision with a car that was already in the first lane. However, the police and Johnny Sr.'s men collided with the oncoming traffic causing a ten-car pileup. Dust and debris from the cars crashing into each other filled the air while Delano merged in with the traffic.

"WHOOOOO SHIT!!!!!" he screamed looking in the rearview mirror and seeing the pileup he'd caused fleeing the scene. He continued to press hard on the accelerator, doing over 100mph on I-94 in his navy-blue Demon Challenger. His car glided smoothly from lane to lane until he got to his destination on the city's Westside.

"MALACHI!!!" Delano screamed as he tried to get help moving Kairo into the house. Malachi was in the living room playing his PlayStation 4 when he heard his father call his name. He peered through the blinds in the windows watching as his father was pulling a badly damaged woman from the front seat. *Is that Kairo?* he thought to himself as he ran towards the door bumping into Nikki walking in the living room.

"What the hell is going on?" she asked, but he didn't know what the hell was going on so he ignored her.

"Excuse me I'm talking to you!" Nikki yelled, pulling on Malachi's shoulder.

"Man, don't fucking touch me. I don't know you," he snapped pulling the door open for his father to bring Kairo in.

"Thanks. Help me run some bath water for her."

Malachi did exactly what was asked of him. He respected Kairo ever since they'd had their little spat back before his father woke from his coma.

"What the fuck is that smell?" Nikki said holding her nose together. She watched as Delano and Malachi took Kairo upstairs for a bath.

"I need a fucking cigarette," Nikki scoffed and walked outside to smoke.

Delano removed all of Kairo's soiled clothes and placed her badly bruised body in an Oatmeal Ginger root bath, giving her the same elixir mix his aunt, The Voodoo Queen, cooked up for his shoulder that Kairo stabbed him in. This healed all scars, removed dangerous infections from the body and healed the skin immediately.

"It-it was Johnny Sr. that did this to-to me" Kairo mumbled, holding onto Delano's arm while he took the warm rag and rubbed it gently against her badly bruised skin.

"Shh, just relax. I promise I'm going to make him pay. I know what he did to your father as well."

"He killed my whole family, my sisters an—"

"He killed your sisters too?"

"Yes, my whole entire family is dead Delano!" Kairo cried, but this was the cost of being the boss.

"Damn!"

"Thank you for doing this for me. I appreciate you not turning your back on me. You're about all I have left," Kairo expressed.

"You're welcome. Despite all the shit we've been through, I still love you. Don't worry, I'm going to kill him for you."

Delano looked at Kairo's bruises below her breasts on her rib cage. Her bruises where so visible you could see the imprint of Johnny Sr.'s brass knuckles. This angered Delano deeply. He couldn't wait to kill Johnny Sr.

"I love you," Delano said.

"I love you too."

While they both confessed their love for one another, Nikki stood outside the door eavesdropping on their conversation. This angered her because she was still in love with Delano as well, but he wasn't in love with her. Nikki wanted to kill this bitch and she was ready to. Kairo was already in a fragile state from the previous torcher. All she had to do was finish her, so she patiently waited until Delano left out the bathroom before making her move.

Right on cue, Delano stepped out to place a call to Johnny. Nikki walked into the bathroom and spotted Kairo in the tub with her eyes closed. *This bitch must die!* Nikki thought to herself as she slowly crept up on Kairo. The floorboards creaked underneath Nikki's footsteps because the house was older, giving away her position.

"Back so soon?" Kairo said smiling, thinking it was Delano returning. When she got no response and felt the shadow of someone standing

over her, she opened her swollen eyes a little and found a very angry Nikki standing over her.

"Nikki what the—"

"Yea bitch, I've been planning this since the day I got back from prison," Nikki said as she tightly gripped Kairo around the neck forcing her to drown. Kairo put up a big fight scratching at Nikki's skin and kicking wildly in the water.

SPLASH! SPLASH!

She struggled with Nikki, trying to do whatever she could to get Nikki to loosen up her grip, but no matter what Kairo did, Nikki wasn't going to let this bitch live. She'd taken everything away from her and she felt the only way she could get her life back was to take it from her.

Kairo kept kicking wildly splashing water everywhere until she could no longer hold her breath. She laid still and gave up trying to fight Nikki from killing her. Nikki thought Kairo was dead and finally left her go. She didn't even bother to check her pulse.

"Bitch, you snooze, you lose," Nikki said before exiting the bathroom. Delano finally returned to the bathroom 5 minutes later not knowing Nikki had just left out. He noticed Kairo was not sitting up in the tub where he'd left her. She was completely submerged under the water.

"KAIRO! KAIRO!" Delano yelled pulling Kairo out the water.

SWEET, STICKY THING

*J*ust a few minutes before...

"Oh shit, I'm about to cum!" Johnny moaned as TJ deep throated him before a call from Delano interrupted his fun time. "

Hold on bae. I got to answer this," Johnny said to TJ who was wiping his mouth from all the slob he'd produced.

"Why are you going to answer that? You were near," TJ huffed folding his arms together. He now had an attitude just like a female when she gets interrupted from sucking her man to a mind-blowing orgasm.

"What's the deal?" Johnny answered, slightly irritated from TJ's funky ass attitude.

"Are you still serious about that one thing?" Delano asked expecting Johnny to remember what was said.

"What one thing?" Johnny was not focused. He was distracted by the shit TJ was saying in the background. He had to zip his pants back up so he could get out the car.

"I am going to kill your father; just give me the location where he's staying," Delano demanded. He was not about to waste any more time searching for this man.

"Alright. Were you still meeting me here at Eastland?" Johnny asked.

"Yea about that, something came up. We gone have to reschedule."

"Oh yea? That's cool."

"I'll catch you around. Send me that address," Delano said before ending the call.

Johnny text Delano his father's address and returned to the car while TJ was *blasting No Love*, by Baby Face Ray. His face was still twisted up because he had an attitude.

"Nigga, what the fuck is wrong with you? You treat my dick like it's your food," Johnny said getting inside the car slamming the door behind him. TJ just continued to stare out the window turning the music up.

"Oh, you trying to be funny. Bitch get out my car! You can walk home!" Johnny snapped.

This made TJ roll his neck with a biting response.

"What the fuck you mean? This is my car."

"Well, you can kindly get the fuck out! Since you want to act like a bitch, I'ma treat your ass just how I treat their raggedy asses. Go on now, get the fuck out!" Johnny demanded, shooing TJ to get out his own vehicle that he paid for every month.

"But I ain't got no way home and its cold out here!" TJ said, calmly getting out the car. He was shocked Johnny would flip on him like that. From the look on Johnny's face, he was serious, and TJ was now regretting his attitude.

"Oh well, figure that shit out. You a nigga. You know how to think with your balls obviously," Johnny said, insulting TJ and making him

feel more like a woman than a man because he was fucking with his mentality.

TJ sucked his teeth.

"Ok, well fuck you too then nigga!" He got out slamming the door and Johnny pulled off. "FUCK YOU!" TJ screamed in the middle of Eastland's parking lot throwing up both middle fingers and sticking his tongue out. As soon as Johnny was out of sight, TJ pulled out his phone and dialed Johnny Sr. He was the reason why TJ knew about Johnny.

"Hello?" Johnny Sr. answered plainly.

"I'm willing to make a deal with you, but you got to pay me all my money on time and I'll deliver your son right in the palm of your hands." TJ spoke into the phone, walking along the parking lot to get to the bus stop.

"Good choice. When can I expect to see you?" Johnny Sr. asked.

"I will call you tonight and let you know. He is pulling back up." TJ disconnected the call before erasing the number from the call log. They both shared the same phone plan, so he didn't need Johnny to be able to pull up cell records. He knew if Johnny ever found out about his betrayal, he wasn't going to live to see another day.

"Man get your bucket head ass in the car," Johnny said as he pulled up on the side of TJ blasting *Accomplishments,* by Cash Kidd.

"Oh, baby this my song. *Aye yo' bitch told me your job interviews ain't been going well, um damn you out here broke as hell,"* TJ said as he was mimicking the lyrics.

Johnny cut the music off.

"Listen to me. Don't ever get no fucking attitude with me." He was pulling on TJ's left ear like he was a child.

"Alright nigga!" TJ whined and rolled his eyes while sitting back in his seat. He was pouting like a kid having a temper tantrum.

Silence filled the entire car between the two, for this was a real awkward situation. They had just gotten into their first argument less than an hour ago and neither of them knew how to reconcile. TJ wasn't sure how he was going to play his hand tonight, so he contemplated the whole rest of the ride whether he was going to betray him or not.

"What's got you so quiet?" Johnny asked, finally breaking the silence between them.

"Nothing." TJ sucked his teeth.

"I'm just thinking about what meat I'm going to cook with the garlic mash potatoes for tonight's dinner."

"Ok, well I haven't had lamb chops in a while. How about that?" Johnny suggested.

"We can do that. Actually, I was thinking the same thing." TJ smiled coldly. He wasn't thinking about anything but that easy ten grand he would get if he betrayed him.

"Maybe we can um, finish what we started earlier tonight in the bedroom," Johnny blatantly said trying to get in TJ's good graces.

"I'm sorry. I have plans tonight."

"Oh yea? With who?" Johnny pulled the car into the white garage. He didn't know TJ had other plans besides being with him that night and this triggered his curiosity. What plans did he suddenly have?

TJ got out quickly, leaving Johnny in the car to avoid the question he'd just asked. He really didn't want to fuck up the plan, so he got dinner started right away to keep him occupied. Then Johnny walked in the house with an attitude, shortly after TJ and said with an aggravated voice,

"Oh, so you just gone ignore my question?" He placed the car keys on the counter and stared TJ in the face. He was waiting on TJ to give him an answer, but TJ didn't have an answer to give, so he had to make something up.

"Kimba and Marley," TJ lied, yanking his neck.

"I don't know them niggas. Who the fuck are they?" Johnny's voice was now getting more hostile watching TJ's careless reaction.

"Before you tune your mouth and say something smart, think about how you say it."

TJ, still ignoring Johnny, went over to the freezer and pulled out a pack of frozen lamb chops before setting it to defrost in the microwave.

"BITCH! YOU DON'T HEAR ME TALKING TO YOU?" Johnny yelled, after he slapped TJ hard across the face. He gasped and touched the bottom of his lip looking at the little blood on his fingers.

"I answered you! I already told you who!" TJ yelled back as he ran the cold water on a clean cloth to keep his lips from swelling.

"You know what? We're not done." Johnny pointed his boney finger at TJ.

"I'm going to take a quick shower. I'll be back down when dinner is ready."

"Yea we gone see about that." TJ mumbled under his breath, not knowing Johnny heard him.

"What was that?"

"I said when these damn lamb chops thaw quick."

"Oh." Johnny nodded his head. He knew that wasn't what he'd heard, but because he didn't feel like coming back downstairs to slap TJ again, he continued to walk up the stairs.

"I'm gone fix his ass! Talking about I can't go nowhere. Watch me bitch," TJ said to himself as he started looking for Benadryl to slip into the Kool-Aid. He scrambled around the whole house looking for it, pulling shit on the floors from the kitchen drawers while slamming the kitchen cabinets and kitchen drawers. Hearing all the ruckus TJ was making became alarming to Johnny and he was now curious about what he was looking for.

"Man, what the fuck is you looking for making all this ruckus?" Johnny questioned.

"Seasonings. I'm sure I'll find it soon," TJ replied getting off his knees from looking under the couch.

"Seasonings? Under the couch?" Johnny shook his head and gave it no thought. He just continued to get his shower started.

After 30minutes of searching, TJ finally found the Benadryl and carefully grinded three pills up before mixing it in Johnny's Kool-Aid. He'd made up his mind he was going to go the fuck out tonight, with or without Johnny's permission. Once the lamb chops were done frying in the air fryer, he mashed the potatoes adding milk, butter and a pinch of salt before stirring it together.

"Dinner is ready!" TJ yelled upstairs, placing Johnny's hot plate of food on the wooden round table. He started eating without Johnny so he could sit back and watch him eat before he passed out.

"Mmmhm, this smells good baby," Johnny said pulling a chair out from underneath the table. He instantly began to dig in eating sloppily, like he'd been starving for months.

"Oh baby, I wanted to apologize about hitting you earlier."

"Mmmhm, yea like you not going to do it again." TJ raised his wine glass full of red Kool-Aid and took a sip to that. He was right. Johnny had a temper and it was no telling when he would hit him again, so Johnny decided not to comment on the abuse he'd given TJ and continued to stuff his face with food.

"Damn, can you slow down?"

"I can't. This shit tastes too good," Johnny replied taking a huge gulp of his Kool-Aid and spilling it from the sides of his mouth.

"Baby, you forgot to stir this. Why does it taste so chalky?" Johnny questioned.

"Oh, um let me stir that up for you." He took the Kool-Aid and stirred it with a spoon. "Here you go. How does it taste now?"

"Better."

TJ sat at the table pounding his fingernails while waiting for Johnny to pass out. He kept looking at his Apple watch as each minute passed by. *Which would be any minute now*, TJ thought to himself. Why the fuck you keep looking at your watch?" Johnny asked.

"I'm going out tonight."

"I thought we already discussed this!" Johnny yelled choking on his mash potatoes.

"Yea, and I'm still going out. Fuck, what you are talking about?" TJ said twisting around in his chair poking his sore lips out.

Johnny was feeling a little sluggish as he tried to reach across the table to grab TJ. He was now feeling the effects of the crushed Benadryl as it consumed his mind and his eyes kept blinking fast as he fought to stay awake.

"Come on, let's get you to bed," TJ said helping Johnny up the stairs to the bedroom.

"Ww-what y-you p-put in that food?" Johnny asked, stammering. He could barely talk; his words were such a slur. TJ tucked him in the bed, pulling the covers over his body.

"Shhh, you need to rest." TJ closed Johnny's eyes that he was fighting to keep open. Now that part was done, he could go get his money.

"AHHH I can hear the money calling my name," TJ said to himself before he stepped out the house to call Johnny Sr.

"Talk to me son," Johnny Sr. answered as if he was expecting TJ to call him soon.

"Ok, I got him to sleep. You can send your men to this address I just texted on the screen," TJ said sternly as his fingers were shivering typing in the address. He knew what he was getting himself into and he was fully aware that he was setting Johnny up to be murdered. Money was the motive to all this. Love wasn't going to pay for that 50,000 surgery he needed.

"Ok I got it. Now meet me at Park Crest Inn on the East," Johnny Sr. said.

"Alright."

TJ grabbed the car keys off the kitchen counter to meet Johnny Sr. in Harper Woods. He drove quickly looking over his shoulders every five minutes just in case Johnny decided to follow, but he knew for a fact the Benadryl had knocked him out cold.

When he finally arrived at his destination, he was a nervous wreck sitting in the parking lot of the Park Crest motel. He couldn't believe he was going all the way with betraying Johnny for money. All he wanted to do was complete his surgery so he could be a whole woman. If he had to scam and scheme to get the money he needed, then that was exactly what he was going to do.

Tap! Tap!

Johnny Sr. tapped gently on the window, startling TJ from his thoughts. He looked up and saw Johnny Sr. staring him in the face. He rolled the window down and Johnny Sr. handed TJ $10,000 in cash rolled tightly in a rubber band.

"I really appreciate this, but you might want your men to get a move on while Johnny is sleep. He will probably wake up in a couple of hours," TJ warned as he turned over the keys in the ignition.

"Well hold on na, this dick isn't going to suck itself," Johnny Sr. said, rubbing on TJ's arm, slightly suggesting that TJ work off that ten grand he'd just handed him.

"Excuse me?" TJ gasped, holding his chest.

"That wasn't a part of the deal! I said I would help you kill your son, not fuck you too!" He wasn't trying to have sex with Johnny Sr. They had never done it before.

"You do what the fuck I tell you to do!" Johnny Sr. yelled, yanking the top of his shirt.

"Fine! I'll suck your dick or whatever you want me to do!"

Fearing that Johnny Sr. might just kill him, he just went ahead and gave in. He wanted to give back the ten grand, but it was too late, he would have to endure this. He should have known better than to trust Johnny Sr.

"What you thought this was?" Johnny Sr. asked.

TJ shook his head in shame and followed behind Johnny Sr. to the motel room. As he stuck the keys in the door, TJ looked around the motel to see if they'd been followed. Johnny Sr. wasted no time zipping down his pants and laying stretched out across the bed. Now Johnny Sr. was no fit man. He was about 5'9 and weighed about 280 pounds with a beer belly.

TJ hesitated to go low on Johnny Sr. because from the looks of it, he had a micro penis. He got on his knees to assume the position, lifting that belly of his to confirm what he was imagining.

"Unt, unt, what the fuck you want me to do with this?" TJ asked, still holding up Johnny Sr.'s stomach. He definitely had a micro penis, no bigger than a woman's clitoris.

The time was now around 4 am when Johnny awoke sweating from his dream. He couldn't tell if the loud boom noise he'd heard was coming from downstairs or his dream. He thought it was just in his dream, but he was indeed hearing things. The Benadryl was now wearing off. *Man, I know I wasn't that sleepy!* he thought to himself when he noticed TJ was not there with him in bed. He got up to use the restroom and heard another loud clash downstairs, this time coming from the living room. Johnny paused in his tracks before continuing to the bathroom

"TJ!!!" Johnny called out but didn't get a response. He rushed over to his safe and punched his code in to retrieve his Desert Eagle.

BOOM!!!!

The intruders kicked open the doors to all the rooms searching for Johnny, but all the rooms they picked were empty. Johnny quietly got up and walked along the wall in his room, waiting for the first nigga to come through the door. He was loaded and ready for whoever came through. Then finally he heard distinct chatter outside the room he was in as they slowly approached the door and kicked it open.

POW! POW! POW!

Johnny let his Desert Eagle rip into their faces before they could step one foot into the room, and blood splattered all over the walls and onto the carpet. He was not about to let them kill him, so he made sure to over kill these two men, shooting 20 rounds in both of them in one spot. Once he was done shooting bullets into their lifeless bodies, he then realized that they both once worked for him. Although they were already dead, he shot them in the head for betraying him. He sat down in the hallway afterwards with the gun in his hand, watching the blood drip from the faces of the two men he'd just killed.

Where the fuck is TJ? Johnny thought to himself before his thoughts were interrupted by a call on one of the intruder's cell phone. He quickly grabbed the phone out their pocket to see who was calling and saw his father's name flash across the screen.

Johnny got up and grabbed his phone off the charger and called TJ, but he didn't answer, so he decided to track him and placed him at the Park Crest Motel on the Eastside. The last call he'd made was to his father at 8pm, right around the same time he was suddenly sleepy. TJ forgot to delete his call history this one time and had finally gotten caught.

Johnny shook his head, refusing to believe that TJ had set him up tonight. It set heavy on his mind that the man he was fucking on a daily betrayed him. This fucked Johnny up and set him back to his old ways. He sat on the ledge of the stairs, lit up a Newport, and waited for TJ to show up.

Shortly, headlights from TJ's car shined through the living room windows bouncing off the ceiling. Johnny remained calm as he smoked through the whole pack of Newports. TJ walked in the house trying to tip toe his way up the stairs but wasn't expecting Johnny to be sitting there.

"Where the fuck was you?" Johnny asked, sitting in the dark puffing on the last cigarette.

"OH SHIT!!! Baby you scared me!" TJ screamed holding his heart. He certainly wasn't expecting to see him sitting next to two dead bodies.

"Do I scare you?" Johnny asked, pointing his Desert Eagle on TJ who was now frightened because he had no idea he was caught.

"Baby! Ahhhhhhh!!" TJ squealed as Johnny smacked him in the face with the gun.

Johnny had red in his eyes, something TJ had never seen before. He was beyond pissed and didn't even waste his time talking. He just looked at TJ and

POW!

"AHHHHHHHHHHHHH!!!!!!" TJ cried as Johnny shot him in the dick. Blood was oozing everywhere, and TJ was holding himself, shocked that a bullet had penetrated his dick. Tears were falling and TJ had slob

running as his mouth held a tight grin. The pain he was feeling was indescribable.

"This is incredulous," Johnny said.

"BABY PLEASE NOOOOO!" He begged for his life, but Johnny wasn't letting up.

POW!

Johnny made another shot killing TJ instantly without hearing his explanation. He didn't want to hear shit he had to say. He hurriedly packed his bags before the police arrived and set the house on fire with all three bodies inside.

13

U THOUGHT WHAT?

"*K*AIRO! KAIRO!" Delano yelled, pulling Kairo out the water to perform emergency CPR. He made light compressions on her chest being careful not to puncture her lungs. He didn't want to damage her no more than she already was. He closed her nostrils and blew his breath in her mouth.

"Come on baby! You can't give up now!" Delano continued to resuscitate Kairo, but her body wasn't giving a response, until finally...

Cough! Cough!

Kairo coughed up the water from her lungs, looking up through her puffy swollen eyes. She was glad to be alive still. If Delano would have stayed out there a little longer she would have died. He looked down at Kairo holding her naked fragile body in his arms.

"Thank God. Are you ok?" Delano asked, continuing to rock Kairo back and forth while sitting in the middle of the sea green and teal tiles in the bathroom. The fragrance of Bath and Body Works Georgia Peach lingered on Kairo's skin and filled Delano's nostrils.

"Yes. I'm fine now, but what is Nikki doing here?"

"She did this to you?"

"Yea, I didn't drown myself, plus I'm cold. You think you could get me somewhere warm and comfortable?" she asked. So, he picked her up, walked into his room where Nikki was sitting on the bed, and before Delano knew it, Kairo leaped out of his grip and onto Nikki.

"BITCH YOU TRIED TO KILL ME!"

"Whoa Kairo! What the fuck!" Delano said, caught off guard at how this escalated so quickly. Kairo gained so much strength onsite.

"Bitch get off me! I thought you were dead!" Nikki said tussling with a very fragile Kairo.

"You thought what?"

PAT! PAT! Kairo landed a few punches in Nikki's face.

"Stop it the both of you!" Delano said getting in between both women. Kairo saw the imprint of Delano's gun on his waist and removed it quickly.

POW! One fatal shot, she intentionally aimed at Nikki's neck.

"AHHH, YOU BITCH!!!!" Nikki yelped as she held her neck. The blood was thick and gushed between her fingers. Nikki was feeling dizzy and collapsed onto the floor, still holding her neck.

"Kairo what the fuck!!!" Delano said as he rushed to Nikki trying to stop the blood from getting onto the tan carpet. But it was too late, blood was already on the carpet soon as her body fell. He couldn't tell if it was because she was being territorial or if it was self-defense.

"Damn Kairo, how many more women you gone kill that I had a past with?"

"The bitch tried to drown me, ok! You weren't there!" Kairo pointed the gun at Nikki's face. She was about to finish her, but Delano stepped in the way.

"Kairo, we can't just be shooting people! She's already about to die. Give me that damn gun!" Delano demanded.

Knock! Knock!

Malachi knocked on the door and entered before anyone could say come in. He peeped his head in to be nosy, only to see Nikki on the floor lying in a pool of blood and Kairo with a gun in her hand.

"Son, I need you to get out of here," Delano said calmly.

"But—"

"I SAID GET THE FUCK OUT NOW!!!" Delano yelled and Malachi listened without trying to talk back.

"Damn! What the fuck Kairo," he said as he applied more pressure to Nikki's throat to stop the bleeding, but it was too late, Nikki was already dead.

"She got what the fuck she deserved, just like Cali!" Kairo screamed.

"SHHH!! Malachi is in the other room. How you think he will feel once he finds out you killed his mother?"

"I don't know. I'm tired of motherfuckas getting down on me! Either you kill Johnny Sr., or I will myself," Kairo said twirling her hands around while pacing back and forth on the carpet.

"Kairo, I will handle this."

Nikki's body was starting to get stiff, each second they contemplated on how they were going to get rid of her. Then Kairo thought to dismember her like they did her father.

"We can use a power saw to cut her up limb by limb and bury her in concrete."

"Hell no! I can't do that to her. What murder shows you been watching? Because that shit sounds heinous as hell! We're talking about the mother of my son."

"I just don't want the bitch to be found. We fucked up with Cali! I'm not trying to fuck up again!"

"Ok listen. Relax. I'll call the Colombians and they will get rid of the body. I got to make a run."

"Delano!" Kairo called out and he turned around.

"You leaving me again?"

Delano paused in his tracks. He did have a pattern. Every time something tragic happened, he left, but it wasn't intentional, it was to seek revenge.

"Baby, you know it's not intentional."

"Well it seems that way, every time!"

"Kairo, you know I'ma street nigga. If I don't kill this nigga tonight, who's to say he won't come back and kill you at any moment?"

Kairo looked to the side and sucked her teeth.

"Well how long will it be before the Colombians get here?"

"Let me place a few calls to Rodriguez and Hernandez. I'll be right back."

As Delano left the house, he called the Rodriguez and he agreed to take care of Nikki for him. He shed a few tears for her and had sorrow in his heart because she was the mother of his child, but that was it. Then he realized he needed to be more comforting to Kairo and headed back inside.

14

NO MORE WORRIES

*T*he next morning, Delano woke up next to Kairo who was sound asleep in his arms. Although she was covered in bruises, she still was beautiful to him in every way. He kissed her forehead before setting his bare feet onto the cold wooden floors. *What the hell?* He thought to himself, forgetting Rodriguez had removed the carpet last night. He looked at his phone and realized he had 11 missed calls from Johnny. He proceeded to go brush his teeth and run a hot shower before calling him back, but Johnny kept calling.

"Johnny, this better be urgent?"

"Nigga it's the only reason I'm calling."

"What's on the floor?"

"Meet me at Northland in an hour."

"Alright nigga. Bye."

Delano ended the call and didn't notice Kairo standing in the doorway. She had her arms folded and studied Delano for a few minutes. Her eyes were no longer puffy, but were still bruised.

"Hey, I didn't see you standing there."

"Why were you talking to Johnny?" Kairo asked. She didn't know he and Delano were working together.

"We are working together."

"Since when? Because the last time I checked, he was going to blow my brains out in our living room back in New Baltimore."

"Kairo, a lot has changed since you've been gone. Please let's not argue."

"We're not arguing, and I've only been gone a couple of days, but help me understand why you're working with the enemy all of a sudden?"

"He is no longer a threat to me. Do you want to take a shower with me?" Delano stepped in and closed the glass door to the shower.

"How could you be so sure? You know he is not trustworthy."

"I trust him."

Kairo had an attitude and she left out the bathroom. This was not making any sense to her. Then she spotted her dead phone on the night-stand next to her. She knew she left it at Michael's, but she didn't know how Delano ended up with it.

"Delano how did you get my phone?" Kairo questioned. He didn't respond because the water was running. She walked into the bathroom and opened the glass door. Steam from the shower escaped.

"How did you get this?"

Delano wiped the water off his face.

"What?"

"How did you get my phone? I left it at—"

"That bitch ass nigga house. I went to go get it."

"Oh."

Delano turned the water off and stepped out the shower.

"If you think I'm trying to betray you, I would never do that. You have no more worries, ok?"

"That never crossed my mind," Kairo lied. She did think for a second that Delano was conspiring against her. The way things were turning out, Kairo couldn't trust anyone. She put her trust in her best friend Cali, she thought, and look where it got her.

"Kairo, I know you thought just a minute ago when I was talking to Johnny that I was against you." Delano sprayed his YSL cologne and got dressed in his Levi's 511's and a plain white tee.

"I just don't trust Johnny or his father!"

"I got you baby. Trust me, I got it handled," Delano said before kissing Kairo on her forehead.

"Let me do my part."

"Ok, D."

"Rodriguez is sending Hernandez and Gonzales to watch over you and Malachi while I make this run."

"Alright. I love you," Kairo said as she watched him walk into his two-car garage.

"I love you too!"

Delano got inside his white 2020 Charge Hell Cat and headed over to Northland Mall in Southfield.

"Damn this is a long ass winter," he said to himself as he backed out his garage. Christmas was approaching soon and so was his birthday on the 24th, but he neglected to go shopping because of all the shit that was going on. He was ready for the holidays and the winter to be over. Within 20 minutes, Delano pulled up alongside Johnny's black Charger, and two men, along with Johnny, joined him inside his car. He pulled his heat out on his lap because he was

leery with new niggas, especially now that he and Johnny were back cool.

What's the deal man?" Johnny said as he got inside peeping the silencer Delano had in his lap.

"Bro, that's not necessary."

"Yea, I don't know these two foreign motherfuckas getting in my back seat."

"Chill. We come in peace. They are my partners Jamal, and his brother Percy. We have a deal to bring to the table."

"Man, we will get to that. What's the deal with your father?"

"That's why I wanted to meet you. As soon as you take my father out, I'm going to assume my position as the Kingpin over Detroit. Once I do that, I'm going to need some product from the Colombians. I'm fucked with the Italians. Marciano is not going to lift a finger to do business with him again."

"You think the Colombians forgot how you fucked them over too?"

"Nah man. See, I know The Don is your grandfather. I'm sure you could look out for me."

Delano looked back at Jamal and Percy as they were nodding in agreeance with Johnny.

"And what do I get out this deal?"

"You could be my partner." Johnny lied through his teeth. He was not interested in sharing his reign with Delano.

"Alright, I'll think about it." Delano sensed Johnny was lying and decided to start keeping a closer eye on him.

"Listen, a new year is approaching. Let's end things on a positive note," Johnny said before exiting the car.

"How do you want your father to suffer?"

"I want that motherfucka to die in the most atrocious way. Make sure you leave no trace of him on this earth."

"Alright."

Johnny scribbled a number on a receipt and handed it to Delano.

"Trace this number to find out where he is and then make your move."

Delano took the receipt and called a guy he knew named Tony as he drove to his storage unit.

"D, waa gwann *(what's up)*," Tony answered in his thick Jamaican accent, inhaling his blunt.

"Yo, I need you to trace a number for me. I need to know his exact location right now."

"Alright. What's de number?"

"586-988-0001."

"Give me a second," Tony said as his fingers click clacked on the keyboard.

"It looks like your dude is at the Mayweather vs Pacquiao fight at the Little Caesars Arena. Oh wait, that's odd. Delano, who are you after?" Tony asked slowly. He knew he was going after Johnny Sr. but if he could avoid a bloody death for Delano, he would.

"Don't worry, I got this."

"You know half the city works for that man! I wouldn't risk it if I were you."

"Well thanks, but I got this."

CLICK!

Delano ended his call with Tony and threw his phone on the passenger seat as he entered his code into the storage unit and pulled up to the large metal doors. He immediately took off his street clothes and

strapped on his bullet proof vest making sure both of his handguns were loaded before placing them in their holsters. He then picked up his bag filled with cutting material and clipped his silencer while rolling a cooler filled with ice and placed it in the trunk before driving to the address Johnny provided him. Within 30 minutes, he pulled up to a gated community where the guard was keeping watch.

"Excuse me sir, we need to see badge for entrance," the tall, skinny guard said. He was dressed in a plain black security uniform. Giles was the name on his badge and he was a geek.

"I have my badge right here," Delano said as he held his silencer low.

"Great. Show me," Giles said unaware that he was about to lose his life just for doing his job.

"Sure."

Pfft!

The silencer was aimed in his face, sending his brains flying in the air. Delano got out the car and saw a green flashing button that allowed him to open the gate. Once the gate opened, he proceeded inside unaware that the cameras were following his every move, something Johnny had neglected to tell him. He knew it would be hard to kill his father, otherwise he would have killed him, himself.

The system alerted Johnny Sr. that a trespasser was on his property and he left his event to go check on his home. A loud noise rang throughout the entire mansion.

"SHIT," Delano whispered to himself as he noticed the red light beaming directly on him. He clutched his silencer in his hand as he walked slowly towards the gunman.

"You wait right there!" The man pointed directly in the center of Delano's chest.

"Who the fuck are—"

Pfft!

Delano shot him and walked into the room where he was sitting with over 30 cameras posted around the house. Each hallway had a camera; even the exterior of the mansion had cameras. He shot all the cameras and stopped when he saw Johnny Sr.'s silver Jaguar arrive.

"Show time," Delano said before shooting the last camera and disappearing to hide.

Johnny Sr. puffed his Colombian cigar and flipped his mink over his shoulders. He could tell his home was violated and someone was still there.

"Come out, come out wherever you are!" Johnny Sr. said as he slowly paced the hardwood floors looking out for the perpetrator.

THUD!

A body went crashing to the floor behind Johnny Sr. He turned around and found one of his men laying on the floor in a pool of blood.

"Ok, whoever you are, show yourself!"

"I'm right here," Delano said coming from his hiding place shooting the other two men Johnny Sr. had as bodyguards.

"Wow!" Johnny Sr. said as he reached for his handgun, but Delano shot him in the arm. "AAHH!!!"

"Don't even think about it. I know what you're reaching for." Delano fired another shot, this time in Johnny Sr.'s kneecap.

"You motherfucker!"

"You killed a lot of people that didn't deserve the treatment you gave them."

"They all deserved what they got, especially that bitch of yours, Kairo!"

"Alright, that's enough talking." Delano aimed the gun at Johnny Sr.'s head while kicking him in the chest with his black heavy-duty boots.

"You ain't gone do shit! You're a pussy just like James raised you to be."

"Why do you keep insulting me? You don't know shit about my father." Delano cocked the silencer.

"Son, I know more than you think." Johnny Sr. shook his head in shame.

"There is something I need to tell you!"

"What?"

"It was the summer of '88 when I met your mother, Gloria. I was searching for a new location to run my prostitution ring and she was married to the man you knew as your father, who was my best friend for years at the time. They had just gotten into an argument and he disappeared. Gloria was a beautiful woman inside out, and I was there to console her. That night, Gloria came down the street, and we had drinks and talked. Shit, then next thing you know, she and I slept together. When she had found out she was pregnant with you, I was already gone. When I got the call, Gloria told me she was pregnant."

"What the fuck are you trying to say?"

"That I'm your biological father!"

"Oh, shut the fuck up. You're only telling me this because you're about to die."

"That is true, but why do you think they separated after all those years? Why do you really think the Northern and Southern cartels were at war in the first place? Your father knew the truth, but he raised you as his own because he didn't want to leave this earth without an heir. You were not supposed to create a child with Cali. She is your sister."

No matter how much Delano didn't want to believe him, it was indeed true, making Malachi his son/nephew and Johnny his younger brother.

"Say your last words before I end you."

"Here is the code to the safe. Inside you will find a manila envelope."

"What's in the safe?"

"Important information you will want to see."

"Take me to the safe." Delano nodded towards the end of the hall where the safe was.

Johnny Sr. got up holding his right arm and limping as he walked to the safe. He punched in four digits and the safe opened.

"This is the envelope I was keeping away from everyone all these years," he said, out of breath from walking.

Delano snatched the manila envelope out his hand and viciously looked through it. He pulled out two sealed documents that were notarized in 89. His birth certificate with his name, his mother's name and his father's, which was Johnny Sr.'s.

"WHAT THE FUCK!! All this shit is falsified!" Delano gasped as he looked at the documents. This angered him deeply and he blacked out.

"I wish it was son, but you are still m—"

Pfft, Pfft, Pfft!

Delano killed Johnny Sr. off impulse, shooting him in the heart three times. He decided he should be headless just like he'd decapitated Kairo's father. So, he took the electric chainsaw out his bag and began removing his head clean off his body. Blood splattered all over the blue walls, getting Delano's clothes messy. Once he removed his head, he placed it inside the cooler on ice.

"What the fuck is this!" He snatched his adoption papers off the table and they confirmed everything Johnny Sr. said. He couldn't believe his

eyes. He was really adopted by James Harris. "This is some sick shit!" Delano said and decided to burn the papers in the fireplace on his way out. Nobody had to know the truth. Things were fine the way they were. Johnny Sr. waited until after all these years to tell him that he was adopted by the man he thought was his biological father. Delano felt no remorse killing him whatsoever. He dialed Johnny to tell him the job was completed and then left to go home.

As he drove, he reminisced on his childhood memories. One night his parents were arguing before they'd gotten divorced.

"I can't believe you would have the audacity to embarrass me like that! You out here dressed like a corner ho," James said as they'd just come in, waking Delano out his sleep. He heard his father's voice boom through the walls and got up to crack the door to his bedroom to be nosey.

"THIS IS ALL YOUR FAULT!!" Gloria screamed as she cried, wiping her tears on her white sheer robe with feather trim. She was wearing a two-piece hot pink bra and panty set underneath, white patent leather 8-inch thigh high boots, and her hair was slicked back into a long ponytail. Delano had never seen his mother dressed up like a corner ho before.

"Gloria, keep your fucking voice down! The boy is in the other room!" James sat at the edge of the couch with both of his hands covering his face.

"We can't live like this! You want to run in the streets all day and leave me here with him days upon days! I got to provide for our son because you gamble all our money away!"

"So the fuck what! I'm the man of this house and what I say goes. Now go take that bullshit off!"

"No!" Gloria stood her ground folding her arms across her chest.

"Woman!" James slapped Gloria.

"What the fuck I just say!"

"Fine, but this isn't over James!"

"You damn right it is. I want a fucking divorce. Let's see who gone help you raise your son then!"

"Fine! Fuck you!" Gloria said throwing her boots at James as he walked out the door. She noticed Delano standing in the crack of the door.

"Come here sweet boy." Gloria motioned for him to come near.

"Everything is going to be alright!" She held him tight. That was the last time he'd seen James until his mother passed.

As Delano parked his car in the garage, he took his boots off and burned everything that had traces of Johnny Sr.'s blood on it. Once he was done, he walked straight upstairs without speaking. Kairo and Malachi were in the living room watching Family Guy and snacking on popcorn. She noticed something was wrong with him as soon as he'd gotten home, so she got up and followed him upstairs. Delano crashed face first into the bed, not knowing Kairo was right behind him.

"Bae, is everything ok?" Kairo asked, standing in the doorway.

"Yea, yea. Come here! She climbed into the bed with Delano and laid on his chest while he caressed her arms.

"Why do I have a feeling you're lying?"

"Baby," Delano exhaled.

"I'm alright."

"Alright." Kairo said nonchalantly. She knew something was bothering him.

"You know what? Let's get married tomorrow!"

"No! Look at me! I have bruises all over my body." Kairo was now self-conscious about her sores.

"None of that matters. I could have the priest come here to marry us."

"You were just going to go to the courthouse?"

"Yes."

"Wait. Did you ever get tested for HIV?"

"Yes. I'm waiting on my results in the mail." Delano lied. He wasn't about to get tested. He knew he didn't have the virus because none of the symptoms ever showed up.

"Ok good," Kairo said falling asleep on his chest as he laid wide awake.

So much was on his mind that he couldn't sleep. *How could this be true?* he thought. *Did I just kill my biological father? Cali is my sister, my son is my nephew, and Johnny is my little brother! I helped kill my sister! Am I HIV positive? What the fuck!!!* Delano tossed and turned in his bed as the thoughts consumed his mind.

Ping!

A text from Johnny came though.

"We need to meet at your club tomorrow at 12pm." Delano rolled his eyes and tossed his phone to the side before finally falling asleep.

15

SAVAGE WAYS

$\mathscr{J}$ohnny sat at the bar drinking shots of Dulce and waiting for his watch to strike 12 pm. He was waiting for Delano to show up so they could discuss business. Now that he was back in charge and his father was out of the picture, Johnny felt good to be running the city's drug trade. He no longer needed to hide, duck or dodge bullets. He needed more product because the feens were going crazy. Crack was their medicine and if they didn't have that rock, then all hell would break loose.

"Do you want another refill?" the bartender asked in a flirtatious tone, breaking Johnny's attention away from the women dancing on the stage. She was attracted to his cologne, the platinum gold that draped around his dark skin, his nicely trimmed goatee and the gold caps he had in his mouth.

"Yea."

She poured him up and slid him her number on a piece of napkin. She knew who he was and how his reputation proceeded him. Johnny found her to be extremely attractive as well, but if she only knew she was barking up the wrong tree.

"Thanks Candice," Johnny said as he touched her soft skin. He looked at the napkin she handed him and put it in his pocket. He was going to use her for something other than sex. The time was 12:05 and Delano hadn't walked through the door yet.

Where the fuck is this nigga? Johnny thought to himself looking at his watch.

Black people could never be on time for shit! Johnny sucked his teeth and decided to watch the girls dance. Although females didn't get him hard, it was nothing like watching bitches twerk and twirl on the pole.

"You want a dance sweetie?" A tall light skin woman whose stage name was Exotica approached Johnny. She wore a peach colored laced bra and panties with black 8-inch snakeskin pumps. Johnny pulled out a stack of $100 dollar bills and a very jealous Candace was looking from afar.

First you get the money

Then you get the power

Respect

Hoes come last

(Oh my God, Ronny)

IGGY AZALEA FT. TYGA'S "KREME" blasted through the speakers. Johnny poured a stack on Exotica. He was intrigued by Exotica's voluptuous body that had tattoos plastered all over her skin. Her long silky blue hair barely covered her double D breasts. Candace was getting jealous watching from afar, neglecting to do her work. Exotica was one of the most highly paid dancers at The Stallion, compared to Candace who was just a bartender. As soon as Exotica straddled Johnny's lap, Candace left from behind the bar.

"Would you like me to take you in the back?" Exotica whispered in Johnny's ear, but before he could respond, Candace spoke.

"Bitch, move! He's mine!"

"Excuse me! Who the fuck is you to come between me and my money?" Exotica snapped walking up in Candace's face.

Candace rolled her eyes and pushed Exotica so hard she lost her balance and fell onto the floor.

"Oh, bitch you dead!" Exotica said as she slowly got back up removing her shoes.

"Ladies, come on. Let's not do th—"

"Fuck that hoe!" Exotica was now running up on Candace. They both got to fighting and weave was being pulled out and thrown every-where. Candace took Exotica by the neck choking her while Exotica dug her nails deep into Candace's skin.

"Biiittcch, let meee go!" Exotica struggled to get free from Candace's grip.

Johnny just sat there unbothered and watched the women tussle until someone came to break them up. He wasn't interested in either woman, but he knew he was going to need Candace. She had some hands on her. Maybe she could knock bitches back into their place if he opened a club. He looked at his watch, the time was 12:30 and Delano still hadn't shown up.

"Fuck this!" he mumbled as he put on his Versace coat to leave. He took his last sip of Dulce and headed towards the door, then Delano finally walked in with a red cooler in his hand.

"My apologies. I got tied up. Let's head to my office," Delano said as he was walking towards Johnny. He'd spent all morning exchanging vows with Kairo in their private garden. Johnny wasn't stupid at all. He noticed the black band around Delano's ring finger.

"It looks like you tied the knot to me," Johnny said following behind Delano to his office.

"Yea. I went ahead and made this life commitment." He looked at his ring as he entered the office and sat the cooler down on his desk.

"There you go." Delano pointed towards the cooler,

"That's what's up man. Congrats! But what's in the cooler?"

"Gone ahead. Check it out."

"Alright," Johnny said rubbing the palms of his hands together. He lifted the lid and saw the head of his father and gasped.

"This some straight savage shit!"

"Yea. You're welcome, but I'm not doing another hit for your ass."

"That's alright, I'll find somebody. Let's get to this money though. Wassup with the Colombians? Maybe we need a new connect for the drugs," Johnny suggested as he closed the cooler and placed it on the side of him.

"Nah, I'm loyal to the Colombians."

"But you see the Colombians are not fucking with me like that, so I got to find somebody else."

"That's true, but who else got a connection?"

"The Koreans! They're cheaper man."

"Hell nah. Fucking around with them niggas might just be sniffing rat poison. Can't afford to have any casualties under our names."

Johnny chuckled and rubbed his goatee.

"Alright. When can you start distributing to the feens on the Westside?"

"I'm not. I'm done with this. As a matter of fact, I'ma move back South," Delano admitted. This took Johnny by surprise. He never expected Delano to give up fast money.

"Alright, well that's your choice. Tell Kairo I said congrats and here is a parting gift," Johnny said giving Delano $5000 in cash.

Ping!

Delano was looking at a text that came though.

"The Colombians have agreed to give you product, but you have to see The Don in person," Delano said as he read the test message out loud.

"Cool. When?"

"Today. They want me to accompany you and they're requiring a deposit of 75 G's."

"Shit. Alright, I got to make a quick run. Meet me at the Detroit Airport at four," Johnny said as he left the club. He had to get a few things straight before he left for Colombia. First, this was a victory that his father was dead, so he stuck the head on a rod and put it in front of his car. He didn't give a damn who saw a dead man's head driving up Eight Mile.

He drove up Eight Mile before making a Michigan U-turn onto Vandyke Ave. *I'm gone show these motherfuckas whose boss!* He thought to himself as he tightly gripped the steering wheel turning right onto Vandyke Ave and speeding through lights cutting in front of whoever was driving slowly. His trigger finger was itching for some fresh blood. He couldn't wait to show his face to all those who'd betrayed him by joining his father.

He pulled up to the warehouse on Vandyke and Lynch and went inside. The female workers were naked and busy talking while packaging the old product. They didn't realize Johnny was walking through the side door. He pulled out his Desert Eagle and shot the lights over their heads. This caught the attention of all the workers,

and they began screaming as they watched light by light being busted out.

"SHUT THE FUCK UP!" Johnny yelled. He was so loud his voice echoed throughout the entire warehouse. He was back to his old savage ways. Being nice made him too friendly. It made the ones he trusted the most turn their backs on him. Now he was there to clean house.

"Where the fuck is Chino?"

"He's not here, but I am," a young cat by the name of Rio said walking into the warehouse. He heard the gunshots and the women's' screams and decided to check it out.

"Who the fuck are you?" Johnny asked. He didn't recognize this young man.

"I'm Rio. Your father put me in charge of the drug ring if something was to happen to him." Rio held out his hand motioning for Johnny to hand over his weapon.

"Well my father is no longer in charge. I am, so you can stop asking for my gun."

"Na homie, you got shit mixed up! Your father was murdered last night so that makes me in charge," Rio said, reaching for his gun but Johnny had already beat him to it.

POW!

Johnny shot Rio right in his chest. The workers didn't make a sound. They stood there and watched Rio's lifeless body go cold on the ground.

"Anybody else want to fucking die?" The women shook their heads no.

"Then get back to fucking work."

Johnny was back and now ready to kill anybody that stepped to him, starting with the niggas who betrayed him. His phone rang and Delano's name flashed across the screen

Ring! Ring!

"What's up?"

"I just got word The Don wants us to be on the way now. If we leave now, we should be there around 6."

"Alright. I'll be on my way." Johnny ended the call.

"Aye clean this shit up!" he demanded.

16

NO LOOKING BACK

airo couldn't stop glaring at this huge rock on her finger. She was now officially Mrs. Harris. The moment she'd been waiting for since she was a child was to be a wife. She wasn't just anybody's wife; she was married to the Kingpin of the South. A bad boy, a drug dealer, a killer but she was addicted to this lifestyle. Bitches died to have the life she'd acquired. Just ask Cali and Nikki. Oh wait, they're dead. Kairo laughed at the thought of those silly rabbits.

BEEP! BEEP! BEEP!

The oven went off, sounding the fire detectors, interrupting Kairo from her fantasy world and bringing her back to reality.

"Shit!!" Kairo screamed forgetting the food was in the oven. Delano called and said he would be getting home late, so she decided to do something nice since they would be spending their first night as Mr. and Mrs. Harris. She planned on cooking this extravagant dinner knowing damn well she didn't know how to cook.

"Malachi!!!" Kairo screamed. She had no clue how to stop the black smoke that was fuming around the kitchen.

"Kairo!" Malachi coughed, looking for the fire extinguisher.

"I'm trying to stop the smoke." Kairo removed the black and burnt turkey from the oven as Malachi sprayed it with the fire extinguisher.

"And my father married you?" Malachi said jokingly.

"What is going on in here?" Olivia, Malachi's girlfriend said as she walked into the smoky kitchen.

"Oh, my goodness! Is that a turkey?"

"Yes," Kairo proudly said.

Malachi and Olivia looked at each other and busted out laughing.

"Your step mama can't cook dawg!" Olivia said still laughing.

"That tickled you huh Liv?" Kairo asked as she stepped away to call the staff back, but another call came through.

"Hello," Kairo answered as she stepped into the family room; the same one Gia was in the night she pulled that stunt.

"Hey Sugar Tits! Long—"

"Don't call me that! I'm married now," Kairo snapped.

"Well I'm sorry to intrude," Michael said.

"I was calling to see when you will be coming back to Beaumont."

"Never! I quit!"

"Wait, hold on. Did you just say you were married?"

"That I did." Kairo was trying to keep it short and sweet.

"WOW! Uh ok! I was checking on you. I haven't heard from you since you left my place.

"You know what? I apologize." She realized he didn't do anything wrong.

"Apology accepted. Wait. Uh, do you have time to see me? It's urgent."

"Not really. What's it regarding?" Kairo asked as she came across the picture of her that Gia wiped with her ass. Silence was on the other side of the phone.

"Hello?"

"Yea, I'm here."

"I asked what it was regarding?"

"It's just better if you meet me. Some shit you just can't talk about over the phone."

"Ok, I'll meet you. Give me a second." Kairo saw something brown smeared on her picture. She picked it up to discover it was smeared shit.

"UGHH!" she screamed and dropped the picture. Next to it was a small camera that Gia had planted a while ago. *What the fuck is this?* Kairo thought to herself as she picked up the camera. It was now dead, but Malachi had one similar.

"Malachi!" Kairo screamed.

"Yes!"

"Can I see your charger similar to this?" Kairo asked. Malachi nodded and ran to get the charger. As she waited on his return, she wondered what Michael could possibly want.

"Here you go!" Malachi returned with the charger.

"Thanks!" Kairo plugged the camera up immediately. *It was dead for a while, so it may take some time to power up,* Kairo thought to herself leaving the camera to charge. She grabbed her Fendi coat and Delano's keys to his Camaro.

"I'll be back Malachi and Liv," she shouted but they were busy playing the PS4. Kairo text her husband that she would be making a small errand with the Camaro and would be right back. He responded quickly telling her it was her car as well and he would be home shortly.

She applied her pink Revlon lip gloss and pulled off listening to *He Be Like*, by Ken the Man. Kairo was happy, watching that rock on her hand gliding back and forth on the steering wheel. She couldn't keep calm as she sped on 94 taking the exit towards Southfield Freeway to get to Michael's penthouse. She pulled up to park in his garage and flashbacks of when she was last here flooded her mind. Digging in her matching Fendi bag, she slid a piece of gum in her mouth to calm her anxiety and got onto the elevator.

Knock! Knock!

Kairo knocked on Michael's door as soon after she stepped off the elevators and he answered within seconds, almost as if he was waiting for her to arrive. When he saw Kairo for the first time since she left his crib, he choked and assumed Delano was beating on her.

"Kairo, is he beating on you?"

"Hell nah! I got into some trouble," Kairo responded, noticing that Michael's place was trashed. She was not used to seeing his place fucked up like this.

"What happened? Why haven't you cleaned up?"

"I've been depressed."

"Depressed about what?"

"Well they found out I was using cocaine and they fired me," Michael said, taking a sip of his favorite cognac Remy Martin.

"Oh wow. How did they catch you?"

"I don't know!" Michael lied. He wanted to save the embarrassing thought of him getting caught sleeping around with a patient.

"So, what's up? My husband will be home any moment now."

"I hope you didn't marry that douche bag!" Michael scoffed.

"Listen, don't insult my husband again. Mind your fucking business!" Kairo snapped.

"Ok I will, but first I need to know if you're going to be a part of my business," Michael said giving Kairo a pretty gift bag. *A gift? What the fuck I do to deserve a gift?* Kairo thought to herself as she opened the bag to find two Clear Blue pregnancy tests.

"Pregnancy tests? What for?" Kairo questioned, forgetting that she did miss her menstrual this month, but she didn't forget about their little fuck fest they'd had almost two weeks ago.

"Go in the bathroom and pee on the stick thingy."

"But—"

"But, it's very possible you're pregnant, so go and take those two tests. I know my sperm is potent and I could produce twins," Michael said cutting Kairo off. She clutched the bag and went to go pee on the stick. She had a million of thoughts that crossed her mind as she sat and waited five minutes for the test to come back negative.

"How is it going in there?" Michael yelled from the other side of the door.

"Um, I'm still waiting," Kairo said, afraid to flip the stick over. Five minutes passed and she hurriedly grabbed the test off the sink. She looked at the words, *PREGNANT 2 WEEKS,* flash on the screen. *Oh, this can't be right!* Kairo thought to herself as she ripped open the next test. How was she going to explain to Delano that she was pregnant by another man?

Knock! Knock!

"How is it going in there?" Michael asked again.

"Just give me one minute!" Kairo screamed and she pissed on the second stick.

"You're pregnant aren't you?"

Kairo opened the door and gave him the second and first test. She was doomed on her own wedding day. It hadn't been a full 24 hours and she was already facing drama.

"Wow! We need to schedule you an ultrasound immediately!" Michael said so happily.

"We don't need to do shit! Are you fucking stuck on stupid?"

"You are going to have my babies!"

"Michael, I don't have to have shit. You better be lucky I'ma let that little comment you just made slide. My husband will murk your ass right where you stand."

"Are you fucking serious right now?" he asked.

"Does it look like I'm laughing?"

"No."

"Alright then. I'm getting an abortion. Fork over $600 to my account."

"You're going to get rid of my twins?" Michael asked.

"What part of I'm married don't you understand? Ok, let that sink in your brain," Kairo said harshly.

"Bitch get the fuck out!" Michael responded finally having enough of Kairo throwing up in his face that she was married. She knew damn well that he had feelings and she just used him like some damn toy.

"Excuse me, wh—"

"I said, bitch get the fuck out!" Michael looked down as he pointed towards the door.

Kairo slapped Michael so hard creating a red mark on his face.

"How dare you talk to me like that?"

"Kairo, GET THE FUCK OUT! Take you and your bullshit across that threshold. Fuck you and that horse you rode in on." Michael pushed Kairo out even though it seemed as if she wanted to argue.

"And I ain't paying for shit, bitch! You figure it out!"

She turned and stood at the door.

"Have a goo—" Michael slammed the door in her face before she could finish her sentence. "Oh god! What the fuck!" Kairo mumbled to herself. She ran to the flowerpot that was outside the elevator and threw up her entire lunch. She got up wiping the corners of her mouth and headed back home to her family.

A very hurt and confused Kairo thought about how she would look pregnant. It was something that crossed her mind, but she knew what to do. As she drove she contemplated on whether to get the abortion or to keep the baby. Finally, she made up her mind she was going to keep the baby and tell Delano about it. As Kairo pulled up, she noticed Delano's car was back from his trip to Colombia. She parked the Camaro and rushed inside to her husband. There he was standing in the kitchen talking to his son and Olivia.

"Hi love!" Kairo greeted Delano cheerfully kissing him on the lips.

"Hello wife. Where you had to go?"

"Uh," Kairo realized she didn't come back with bags.

"I left to go to CVS but I didn't see anything I wanted."

"Ok, I was just talking to the kids. I heard you were burning down the kitchen."

"Um yea, Malachi put it out. You think you could meet me upstairs in 30?"

"Sure," Delano replied.

Kairo walked upstairs and lit the candles she'd found. She also lit some incense and put on some soft R&B music. Kairo looked through her new lingerie drawer Delano purchased for her the other day from Savage X Fenty.

"He would like this!" she said as she held up a lavender lacy one-piece.

Knock! Knock!

Delano didn't wait the full 30 minutes like Kairo asked. He was ready to consummate their marriage. He walked into the room while Kairo still was holding the lavender lingerie in her hands and she turned around, surprised he came upstairs so quickly.

"Babe, you were supposed to wait 30 minutes," Kairo said, putting down the lingerie.

"Yes I know, but I missed you and I couldn't wait to consummate our marriage."

Delano held onto Kairo's shoulders kissing her on the lips. He really missed the way she felt. He began caressing her breasts through her shirt removing it over her head. Kairo's breasts were larger than normal, but that didn't stop him from sucking on her nipples as they stood in the middle of the room.

"Oh, I miss the way you suck on them," Kairo moaned.

"Mmmhm," Delano said, picking Kairo up and taking her to the bed. He spread her legs wide and noticed her pink pussy was already glistening. He licked her pussy so good, she came in his mouth twice and she twitched as an orgasm erupted through her body.

"OHHH I'm about to squirt!!!" Kairo moaned holding onto Delano's head as her warm juices created a waterpark on his face. He inserted two fingers and fingered her juicy pussy until she creamed in his hands.

"Oh shit, that feels good!" She move her hips in a circular motion as she watched him lick her dry.

"You like that baby?" he asked, getting up and removing his shirt while Kairo ran her hands over his muscular chest. His dick was throbbing. He hadn't had pussy in so long he was gone tear her pussy down. He inserted himself deep into Kairo, grinding inside her while kissing her on the neck. Kairo moaned and closed her eyes as she got lost into the music while Delano made love to her. This took her to another level, making her forget about Michael and the pregnancy.

"Damn, this pussy is so fucking wet!" Delano said as he gripped tightly onto Kairo's ass going deeper inside her. She was wetter than the ocean and creamier than the middle of a hostess cupcake.

"Baby I love you so much," Kairo whispered in his ear. He quickened his pace pounding Kairo's pussy until she squirted again, this time tightening her muscles around the girth of his penis.

"I love you too!" he said.

"Now turn that ass around."

Kairo got on her knees as Delano slapped her ass and kissed each cheek before entering inside her. Her breasts dangled on the pillows, creating friction with her nipples. She liked the feeling of her nipples rubbing against the pillows while he pounded her out. He grabbed her shoulders and shoved all 8-inches deep inside her while she tightened her muscles.

"Fuck baby, you gone make me nut inside you!"

"Do it daddy. Cum inside this pussy!" Kairo said so loud that Malachi and Olivia overheard them. They giggled at the adults because they were loud as hell.

CONSEQUENCES

"*D*amn. That's how your parents get down?" Olivia asked, smacking on her gum while naughty thoughts clouded her young mind.

"Hell yea. They used to fuck all day every day," Malachi replied as his eyes stayed glued on the game that was in front of him.

"That's how we need to be," Olivia said removing her white top exposing her young breasts in her navy-blue bra.

"Whoa Liv. I thought you said you wanted to wait?"

"Fuck that. I'm horny now!" Olivia said, leaning over on Malachi rubbing on his dick.

"Alright, go lock the door."

Olivia got up and twisted her thick hips in her plaid mini skirt over to the white door, locking it. She turned around slowly, un-clamping her bra and biting her bottom lip. Her perky B-cup titties aroused Malachi, causing his dick to rise in his Versace drawers. She walked over to him slowly before straddling him and pushing him back onto the bed.

"Your dick is hard as hell right now," Olivia said as she dry humped him in her navy-blue cotton panties. Malachi plopped both of Olivia's brown erect nipples in his mouth allowing his hands to run freely over her smooth body.

"Oh, suck on these titties baby!" she whispered as she let out a small moan.

"Come here," Malachi said switching roles with Liv. Now she was on her back while he went down on her. He lifted her plaid mini skirt, pulling her panties down and exposing her lightly trimmed bush. Malachi was turned on by Olivia's natural scent and her bush. He never had a girl whose pussy wasn't shaved. She would be his first.

"Wait, wait!" Olivia said. She was anxious but nervous at the same time. She was a virgin and had never been penetrated before. She was only 16 and wanted to wait until she was married, but she wanted to experience sex with her boyfriend now.

"What's the matter?" Malachi questioned.

"I think I'm ready."

"Uh, are you sure? Because I'm ok with us kidding around," Malachi asked.

"Yes, baby please!" Olivia said spreading her legs. She was tired of Malachi teasing her with his tongue. She wanted to experience the real thing so she could go back to school and have something to talk about with her girls.

"Alright. Let me get a condom."

"No, it's fine." Olivia said grabbing Malachi by his arm.

"Let's have sex raw."

"Ok."

Malachi knew she hadn't been with anybody, so he didn't think twice about any outcomes. This was also his first time with a virgin. He'd

fucked plenty of loosy goosy hoes in South Eastern, but she was his first virgin.

"Baby, are you sure?" Malachi said staring into her eyes after he licked her pussy to get wet for him to enter.

"Yes, I am sure!" Olivia said closing her eyes as he entered her. Malachi was packing just like his father with 7 inches of thick dick.

"Ah, ah, ah," Olivia moaned. She could feel her hymen being torn down as he took his time planting kisses on her skin.

"You ok?" Malachi asked before he began stroking her. He wanted to be sure she was comfortable. She nodded and kissed him.

"Alright, just stop me when you're ready."

"Baby, fuck me already!"

Malachi did slow strokes inside Olivia, kissing her soft skin. She was light skinned just like him. He licked and sucked on her titties while he was grinding in her pussy just like his favorite porn star, Xavier.

"Fuck baby, you feel so damn good!" Malachi had never had pussy so good before. He went deeper inside her, reaching an orgasm.

"Oh, shit!"

"What?" Olivia jumped up.

"I came inside you," Malachi said taking his dick out that was covered in blood.

"That's ok. We can get a Plan B."

"No, let's wait and see first."

"See wh—"

Knock! Knock!

Olivia's words were interrupted from the two knocks at the door and they both froze once they heard Kairo's voice.

"Malachi, how do you turn on this camera thingy?" She twisted the doorknob.

"Why is your door locked?"

"UHH," he stammered. They both rushed to put their clothes on, but Kairo knew what was going on. After it took them three minutes to straighten up, he finally opened the door. Kairo stood at the door with her arms folded. She could smell the sex linger out the room.

"What were y'all doing? I smell sex," Kairo said as she walked into his room and realized it was blood stains on his bed sheets.

"We were just playing the game," Malachi lied. He knew they were fucked.

"Hey, you ain't got to lie to me. Did y'all use a condom?"

"No, it was Liv's first time." He held his head down ashamed that he'd just lied to his stepmother.

"Look up Son. That is nothing to be ashamed of, but I'ma let your father handle this. Come on in here. You too young lady." Kairo motioned the teenagers down the hall to their room.

"What's going on? Delano asked, looking up from his phone.

"Go ahead and tell us what happened." Kairo sat down on the edge of the bed, crossing her legs and folding her arms.

"What happened?" Delano's facial expression changed. He was suddenly confused about what was going on.

"Son, cat got your tongue?"

"No sir."

"So, what happened?"

"Liv and I had sex and we didn't use protection," Malachi confessed.

"Oh, that's it? I thought you were going to say you robbed a bank." Delano jokingly said trying to lighten the mood.

"Son look up. There is nothing to be ashamed of. And young lady hold your head up," Kairo said holding her head up.

"Listen, we've been fucking since we were teenagers ourselves. Not saying I condone you having sex in my house, but you are exploring and I understand that. Now, did you finish?" Delano asked.

"Yes."

"Did you pull out?" Kairo asked, chiming in.

"No," Malachi said, shaking his head.

"Ok. Liv do you know the factors of STD's and teenage pregnancy?" Delano asked.

"Yes, I'm well aware," She shyly responded.

"Ok," Delano said pulling out a stack of condoms handing them to Malachi.

"How would your parents feel if you were pregnant right now? Who is going to help you raise the baby?"

"I wasn't going to tell them," she admitted.

"Ok, that's enough. We are about to get a Plan B right now," Kairo said grabbing her Fendi purse.

"Come on. Don't stand there. Go get your coats."

"Alright baby, you got this? I got to meet up with Johnny," Delano said as he put on his Burberry coat and his Cartier wood frames.

"You know I can't stand that man," Kairo said.

"Yes baby, I know." He kissed her on her forehead.

"Alright just be safe! Text me when you make it safely. I love you."

"I love you too!" Delano kissed Kairo on the lips before departing to meet Johnny.

He grabbed the keys to his Hell Cat and drove to The Whitley's on Woodward. As he drove, he couldn't help to think Kairo's pussy was super wetter than normal. *She must be pregnant,* he thought to himself because he knew what pregnant pussy felt like. *But if she's pregnant, whose baby is it? Because it's been a while since we've been intimate.* Delano stopped thinking and concentrated on the road. It was going to drive him crazy if he assumed white boy had gotten her pregnant. As Delano drove, the snow began to fall heavily making it hard for him to see. He turned on his favorite Detroit rapper Cash Kidd to ease his thoughts.

Ring! Ring!

A call from Johnny came through and he answered.

"What's the deal Johnny?"

"How fast can you get here?"

"Nigga I'm in route. The snow is falling heavy as fuck in the streets.

"Alright, make it quick. When you get here come straight to the back in the private section," Johnny said before disconnecting the call. Delano arrived within 15 minutes and headed straight to the back just like Johnny asked him.

18

BLOODY JOHNNY

"Will that be all for you gentlemen tonight?" the waitress said with her pen and pad in her hands taking the orders down. Johnny nodded and so did the others in agreeance. Delano walked in and sat his coat on the back of the wooden chair.

"Sir, you can order whenever you're ready."

"Yea, order whatever you want. It's all on me," Johnny said to Delano as he held his hand up to his mouth pondering and watching the seven men that had betrayed him sit at the same table with him.

"I'm ready to order," Delano said, and the waitress waited on him.

"Can I get a lobster bisque?"

"Sure. Coming right up," the waitress said as she walked away.

Delano knew Johnny was up to no good, so he leaned in and asked him.

"What the hell is going on?"

"Watch and see," Johnny replied.

The men were having such a good time conversing amongst each other, that they neglected to pay attention. Whenever Johnny was quiet and didn't engage in conversation, he was up to something. Delano had no idea what was going on in Johnny's mind as he sat there watching the seven men laugh and crack jokes.

"Man, Johnny I never knew you to be so generous. What's the special occasion?" Scar asked. He was a short pudgy motherfucka with a large gash running across his face from years ago, which is how he acquired his street name.

"I just wanted to be generous. I know y'all weren't expecting me to return."

"Hell nah. We just knew your dad was going to take you out!" Rudy said. He was the least bright of them all. Johnny chuckled. He knew this dummy didn't just confess he knew about his father trying to take him out the game.

"You know what Rudy, you got to be the dumbest motherfucka I know!" Chino said, making the other men focus on Rudy. The waitress brought out their food and placed it in front of them. Johnny didn't touch his plate and Scar noticed.

"Boss you not gone eat?" Scar asked.

"I'm not hungry."

"Ok, well when are we gone start with our new product?" Chino asked.

"There will be no product for you to touch," Johnny said coldly cracking his knuckles. He finally had a plan on how he was going to deal with these traders.

"Then what the fuck did you call us here for?" Prune asked. He was a skinny ole prune ass nigga from Six Mile.

"It has been brought to my attention that you all, except my buddy Delano, has betrayed me."

The men stopped eating and all eyes were on Johnny as he stood up and walked around the table. The room grew quiet and the laughter stopped.

"Boss none of us meant to betray you," Scar said.

"I know. That's why I brought you all here, so you can enjoy your last meal."

"Fuck this! I'm out," Ralph, Rudy's twin brother said. He stood to leave, throwing his white cloth napkin in his plate of food.

"SIT THE FUCK BACK DOWN!" Johnny yelled, but Ralph kept walking. As soon as his hand touched the doorknob. *POW!* Johnny shot him, sending him to meet God before his time. "Anybody want to follow his footsteps?

"Naw boss. We good," Rudy said as he watched his twin brother's brains being blown to smithereens.

"Good. Now I need help digging your graves or you too can die with a bullet."

"Don't you think you're being a bit too extreme?" Rocky finally spoke up and said. He was quiet this whole time and should have remained quiet. Johnny didn't even answer him. He just shot him in the face, killing him instantly.

"Anybody else?"

The remainder of the men shook their heads no because they knew what time it was. Delano sat there observing each man's face and could smell the fear rolling out their pores. He wasn't clear on to why Johnny called him there. He hadn't betrayed him.

"I want each and every one of you to follow me outside really quick," Johnny demanded. He was serious as a heart attack.

"You don't need to do anything but watch," he said stopping Delano in his tracks. The rest of the men followed Johnny outside to his van where he handed everyone a shovel.

"You're all going to need these."

"Wait, what do we need these for?" Rudy asked. He was dumb as a box of rocks. Johnny mentally noted to kill him first.

"Shut the fuck up Rudy, or you'll end up like your twin," Luka said. He didn't speak much because he knew they all were going to die for betraying Johnny.

"Now that you all have your shovels, step inside the fucking van," Johnny commanded. They quickly got inside, leaving behind their coats, cars and cell phones.

"Man, where the fuck are we going?" Steven asked. He was another quiet one but couldn't help but to ask about a location.

"Just sit the fuck back and ride," Scar responded.

Johnny closed the back of the doors and told Delano to ride with him down to Woodland cemetery. As they drove, the men began to chatter amongst themselves. They knew they were fucked and couldn't escape from the hands of Johnny's revenge.

"Those men you see back there betrayed me and now they must die. Any suggestions on how I should do this?" Johnny asked Delano.

"Just shoot them execution style. No traitor should live."

"No duck, duck goose?"

"Man, fuck naw. Straight execution style."

"Alright, cool." Johnny pulled to the back of the cemetery that he'd purchased just for this moment, and parked opening the back of the van.

"I want each of you to stand side by side and dig."

"We're digging our own graves?" Chino asked.

"The fuck it look like nigga?" Johnny said, aiming the gun in his face to cause intimidation.

The men began digging and removing the snow that covered the ground. They dug for two hours without stopping, and they were freezing cold because they left their coats back at the restaurant.

"We're fucked!" Rudy said. He was just realizing that he was digging his own grave.

"No nigga, you're fucked. I know who killed his sister, California," Scar said looking up to see if Johnny was overhearing their conversation.

"What nigga? Who?" Rudy asked. He was on some grimy shit and Scar could tell, so he lied and told him it was Delano.

"Boss, boss!" This caught Johnny's attention.

"What is it Rudy?"

"I got some information on your sister, California," Rudy happily said because he thought this was going to be his ticket out. Johnny was all ears. He was elated to hear about his sister who'd mysteriously disappeared from the earth.

"I-I know who killed your sister!"

Now while Rudy was busy snitching, Scar told the other men.

"Watch this slow ass nigga." They stopped digging and watched.

"That's who killed your sister!" Rudy pointed towards Delano. He didn't even know his name; he was just trying to live. Delano looked up and saw Rudy accusing him of Cali's death. Although it was partially true, Johnny didn't believe Delano would kill his own baby mama.

"Really? Where's your proof? Who told you this?" Delano questioned walking towards Rudy while Johnny stood there.

"I got it from Scar!" Rudy was choking on his words.

"So, you don't have any real proof. You're just out here accusing motherfuckas?" Johnny questioned.

"No."

"Delano—"

Before Johnny could give the order, Delano didn't hesitate. He pulled his pistol from his waist and *POW! POW!* Shot Rudy right into his grave. Then he turned the gun on the rest of the men, shooting them all except Scar because he was out of ammunition.

"Whooaaa, somebody is trigger happy!" Johnny said as he aimed his gun at Scar to shoot.

"Wait!! I really know what happened to your sister!"

"What!?" Johnny said.

"If you allow me to live, I'll bring you the heads of the killers."

"Killers?"

"Yea. It's more than one," Scar said cutting a grudged eye at Delano. He knew something and Delano could tell just by the dirty look he gave.

"Alright. Come on," Johnny said helping Scar out the grave.

"You better not be on no bullshit either, or I will kill you." They got into the van and headed back to the restaurant. The whole time as they were driving Delano was wondering who the fuck was this nigga's source. He had a dangerous problem on his hands now, and he had to solve it and get rid of it.

"Yo, Johnny you good? It's getting late and I need to get back home to my wife," Delano asked as they got back to the restaurant.

"Yea go home back to your wife. I got to see what the fuck Scar knows about California's disappearance."

"Alright nigga. I'll see you around." Delano walked away and got inside his Charger. He closed the door and immediately dialed Tony. He needed more information on Scar so he could silence him before he talked.

"Ya man," Tony answered, inhaling his blunt as always.

"I need you to look into a nigga named Scar for me. I'ma call you back when I get more information."

"No problem," Tony said before ending the call.

It took him no more than 15 minutes to get home. He walked into the kitchen, flipped on the light switch, removed his boots at the door and Kairo came rushing down the stairs. She'd heard him coming because his loud music shook the entire house.

"Hey baby, I didn't know you were still up. Did I wake you?" Delano asked, putting the keys on the key ring. Kairo's eyes were clearing up, but he was still able to see she had been up crying.

"Baby what's wrong?"

"Can you tell me what this video is?" Kairo asked. She'd finally had the chance to watch the video. She couldn't get pass the part where Gia confessed that she was a man, but had she just continued to watch it, she would have seen what happened.

"Where the fuck did that camera come from?"

"Your family room. Did you do anything with this man?"

"What!?" Delano was offended. He'd never displayed any gay behavior.

"You didn't finish watching it?"

"No."

"If you would have finished, you wouldn't have even offended me with that bullshit," Delano said walking up the stairs and Kairo followed behind him. He was right. She should have just finished watching the video.

"Besides, I killed him. Do you not trust me?"

"I never said I didn't trust you," Kairo said, finishing up the video.

"Man, get that shit out my house. I'm going to sleep. It's been a long ass night," Delano said running the hot water in the shower. Kairo continued to watch the video, dismissing the accusations she'd had in her mind. She knew she was wrong for accusing him, but she's just a lot on her mind since earlier.

"I'm sorry baby. I apologize for accusing you for sleeping with that man."

"You're straight. Just don't ever in your life think I would have sex with another man." Delano turned around allowing the hot water to beat on his skin and scrubbing every inch of his body with his dove body wash. He lathered his rag before rubbing it across his chest and hitting his other main body parts.

"I got a surprise for you," Kairo said as she joined Delano in the shower.

"Really bae?" Delano turned around facing Kairo in the shower.

"Yea, I got it earlier when I took the kids to CVS. Think of it as a wedding gift."

"Ok, I'll open it after I eat your pussy in this shower." Delano turned the shower head the other way so that he could bury his head down below.

"Baby, I'm tired and ready to go to bed," Kairo said stopping Delano from going down on her.

"What? You don't want me to lick you until you cum?" Delano was surprised she turned down his head.

"No, I'm not really in the mood to do any of that." Kairo stepped out and dried her body with the peach towel. She was thinking about Michael and the baby. Delano could see something was really bothering her, so he asked.

"Is this about the tranny that tried to get me to fuck her?"

"No. I just miss my family," Kairo lied trying to mask her real thoughts. She did miss her family. After all, they were killed by the hands of Delano's enemies. They were not her enemies until he came back into her life. She laid there crying silently because she was emotional.

"Awe bae, things will get better I promise," Delano said kissing Kairo's forehead.

"Oh, I almost forgot," Kairo said reaching in the nightstand pulling out a medium gift box.

"Babe don't be buying me stuff. You know how I feel about that."

"Yes I do. Now open it."

Delano opened the navy-blue box that said ROLEX written in all caps inside. His watch was black encrusted with Gold and Platinum diamonds around the watch face. He picked up the price tag and saw it said $15,000. He almost shitted himself. He'd never had a woman spend that much on him, ever.

"Baby, where you get all this money from?"

"I got it out my savings," Kairo said, which was partially true. She also used the cash Michael wired for the abortion and for an apology while they were getting the Plan B at CVS. Money can't buy love, especially not Kairo's.

19

CHRISTMAS EVE

"You know it doesn't make much sense,

There ought to be a law against

Anyone who takes offense

At a day in your celebration

'Cause we all know in our minds

That there ought to be a time

That we can set aside

To show just how much we love you

And I'm sure you would agree

It couldn't fit more perfectly

Than to have a world party

On the day you came to be

Happy birthday to you

Happy birthday to you

Happy birthday."-Stevie Wonder

"HAPPY BIRTHDAY!" Delano awoke to Malachi and Kairo screaming happy birthday while playing Stevie Wonder's version of the Happy Birthday song. He was sleeping well until they came into the room waking him out his deep sleep. He looked over at his clock and saw that he'd slept late. He sat up in bed and rubbed his hand over his face still trying to adjust to the lighting in the room.

"Thanks guys!" Delano said, wiping the cold from his eyes and squinting trying to wake up completely.

"Good. Get dressed because I have surprise for you," Kairo said as she kissed his cheeks.

"Ewww! Y'all get a room. Oh, can I invite Liv?" Malachi asked.

"Sure," Delano responded getting out of bed. He was just turning the big 30 and felt like he was still 29. Age really didn't mean shit to him. All he cared about was getting Scar's head on a silver platter.

"Baby, we have reservations tonight at Texas Roadhouse on Twelve Mile and John R," Kairo said as she left the room to take a shower. That was Delano's favorite restaurant and he appreciated his wife for making plans, but he needed to hit the streets. He dialed Johnny's cell and got the voicemail.

"What the fuck," Delano said as he attempted to dial Johnny one more time, but Johnny's call came through.

"Yo, wassup?" Johnny spoke into the phone coughing.

"So tell me, did you hear anything on Cali?" Delano asked. He looked over his shoulder to make sure Kairo was not in the room.

"I gave him two days to get his facts straight."

"I think he is lying. He don't have no proof about who killed your sister."

"How can you be so sure?" Johnny questioned.

"Bro, she's been missing for months now. Why didn't he tell you before now that he knew who killed her? He's just trying to buy time," Delano said.

"That may be true. He might be bluffing."

"You don't think so?"

"Man, I tell you what, you go ahead and enjoy your birthday and let me worry about Cali."

"Alright." Delano ended the call. He turned around and Kairo was drying her wet body off with her peach towel.

"Who was that?" she asked.

"Johnny."

Kairo rolled her eyes and scoffed at his name. She truly didn't trust Johnny. Because of him and Cali, her mother was dead. She was so sick of her husband not trusting her instinct that he was no good, so she would just have to deal with their newfound friendship.

"What time is dinner?" Delano asked as he kissed Kairo on the lips.

"Six."

"Good, it's only four. You got some time to play?" he asked sucking on her neck.

"Oh baby, you are being bad again."

"Fuck yea. Come here. You smell so damn good," he said, pulling her closer to his body. Inhaling the sweet Warm Sugar Vanilla scent that lingered on her skin, he sucked on her breasts like a hungry baby, teasing both of her nipples with the tip of his tongue before the whole areola disappeared in his mouth. He picked up Kairo and laid her back

onto the bed, removing his wife beater. Seeing that Kairo was already wetter than the Pacific Ocean, he inserted himself and positioned her legs over her head.

BANG! BANG!

The headboard clashed against the wall as he pounded aggressively enjoying the sweet bliss. Her pussy was so wet, Delano knew she had to have been pregnant. He let Kairo's legs down in the missionary position and stroked deeper. She kissed him and moaned while he made sweet love to her for an hour.

"I love you Kairo," he said rolling over after he'd just busted inside her.

"Do you?" Kairo jokingly questioned turning on her side with her hand holding her head up. She loved Delano too but he stayed in the streets too damn much.

"Yea, I do. You wouldn't be getting dicked down as good and you wouldn't have my last name if I didn't love you."

"You stay in the streets more than you stay home," she finally had the courage to say.

"Baby, the streets is how we eat," Delano said getting up to take a shower.

"Ok."

"Can we enjoy Christmas Eve?" Delano asked as he handed Kairo a huge box wrapped in shiny red wrapping paper.

"Oh, this is for me? Isn't it your birthday?" Kairo asked taking the gift and ripping the paper off the white box. She thought it was another pair of shoes, but it was a brand-new black Birkin bag made of snakeskin.

"OH MY GOSH BABY! THANK YOU!!!!" Kairo squealed.

"Look inside," Delano said smiling to see the joy on her face.

Kairo slowly unzipped her new purse and found another small box along with the $15,000 in cash she'd spent on his Rolex. Kairo shook the box before opening it and it was another box. This time she opened another box with a key inside.

"Oh, what is this key to?" Kairo questioned.

"I'll reveal it during dinner."

Kairo was so grateful for her gifts that she decided to return the favor and surprise him at dinner. As Delano showered, she went downstairs and took another pregnancy test. She got the same results as before and wrapped it up inside a mini gift bag. She knew she wasn't shit; she just didn't want to go through with the procedure. Michael would be pissed once he found out that Kairo had never gotten the abortion. Instead, she used the money towards Delano's Rolex.

The time was now 6pm and they'd just arrived at Texas Roadhouse. It was overcrowded as always making it difficult for Delano to find a parking spot, so he ended up parking further away from the door. They exited the car and were seated inside their booths.

"Can I just say how much I appreciate being here with you guys?" Olivia confessed breaking the silence at the table. They were busy looking at their menus when Olivia spoke.

"You're welcome Liv," Kairo said smiling.

"Baby, I'm ready to order. Are you?"

Ping! Ping!

"Yea give me a second," Delano said looking at his phone. Tony texted him the info he requested the other day about Scar.

"We got to go."

"No, wait! We just got here!" Kairo whined. This made Delano feel a little guilty, so he decided to stay put.

"Thank you!" She returned to looking at the menu. She was borderline upset that Delano allowed the streets to come between their times together.

"Oh, since we're waiting, here is my gift for you." Kairo pulled out the blue mini bag and handed it to Delano.

"Wow! You're pregnant?" Delano said trying to sound excited. He already knew she was pregnant. This just confirmed it.

"Congrats!" Malachi and Olivia said at once smiling.

"Thank you family! Now are you gone tell me what this key goes to?" Kairo asked, holding the key in the palm of her hand. She'd been itching to ask him about it since they were back at the house.

"Oh yea." Delano pulled out a paper from his back pocket.

"This here is your blueprint to your new boutique called Chronic." He sprawled out the blueprint for them all to see.

"You're looking at your store that will open January 1st, 2020."

Kairo was speechless. She couldn't believe Delano went out his way and purchased her a building. Not only did she have a building, but she was now a boutique owner.

"Did you say January 1st?" Kairo asked to be sure she'd heard him correctly. He nodded and flashed a smile.

"But I don't have any inventory!"

"I already got you taken care of. Don't worry about that!" Delano said showing her a catalog in his phone of the clothes that she would be selling. He didn't tell her the truth about why he'd given her the boutique in the first place. All she saw was a blueprint and a key. She didn't know he was going to use this business to clean his money and smuggle drugs through her shipments.

"Oh my goodness baby! Thank you!" Kairo said. She was more than grateful to have a husband like Delano. He had his perks being a good man, but he was a street nigga at heart.

Ring! Ring!

Tony called Delano back to back. He tried his hardest to ignore the first call, but when Tony called again, he knew it had to be important.

"Hold on," he said to Kairo as he took the call. He excused himself from the table and stepped outside.

"What's up Tony?"

"Yo' boy Scar is on to you and Kairo. You might want to get a move on ASAP."

"What happened?"

"You know I never reveal my sources, but you better get to him before he gets to Johnny."

"Alright." It was no more talking. Delano was feeling the fire in his veins. He returned to his table and told his family.

"It's time to go now!"

20

JOHNNY, JOHNNY

*R*ing! Ring!

"AGGGHHH what the fuck!" Johnny said as he rolled over from taking a nap. He looked at his phone to see who was calling him back to back like this. He had one eye open squinting to see the number that appeared on top of the screen. It was a very familiar number so he finally answered.

"Hello?"

"I got what you're requesting," Scar said coolly. He was amped and wanted to share.

"Alright. Meet me at my warehouse in an hour."

"Cool," Scar said as he ended the call.

"Huh, shit!" Johnny sighed as he finally found the strength to get out the bed. He looked at himself in the mirror, noticing how sickly he was starting to look. Soon the virus was going to turn into AIDS, if it hadn't already. He thought back on the time when he was first diagnosed with HIV.

"Johnny, I know you're only 16 and this is going to be a hard pill to swallow, but do you have any clue as to who gave you HIV?" the doctor asked.

"I think I have an idea of who it may be," Johnny responded with tears in his eyes. This was the most painful thing he'd ever heard in his life. He was only 16, parentless and had been in and out of different foster homes since he was 11. He'd only had California and she was also gone into the system. He just knew the one person whom he loved and cared about hadn't just given him HIV.

"That Goddamn Kareem," he said to himself as he shook his head.

"I'm sorry, did you say a Kareem?" the doctor asked.

"Yea, he's my boyfriend," Johnny responded nonchalantly.

"Ok, if you want you can report him to the CDC an—"

"Why the fuck would I do that?" Johnny said before storming out the hospital. He needed answers, so he pulled up to Kareem's house in the King Homes. He went to park his car directly in the same spot as always, but today there was another car in his spot.

"Who the fuck's car is that?" Johnny said to himself. He parked his car next to Kareem's Tahoe.

Knock! Knock!

Johnny knocked on the green door and got no answer. He heard somebody scrambling on the inside.

"What the fuck?" He peeped in the kitchen window and saw someone hiding. Shortly after, Kareem answered in his robe with his hairy chest out.

"Babe, what a pleasant surprise. You didn't tell me you were stopping by," Kareem said caught by surprise. Johnny already knew he was up to no good, so he pushed Kareem back into the door.

"Move! Where the fuck is that nigga?" Johnny asked as he peeped Kareem's 9mm. on the kitchen table.

"Wait, who are you talking about?" Kareem closed the door.

"Don't fucking play with me! I know he is around here some fucking where!"

"Johnny put the gun down! You're acting irrationally!" Kareem screamed.

"Irrational bitch! You gave me HIV and I'm irrational?" Johnny admitted.

"What!" Kareem screamed. From the sound of it, he was unaware he had the virus himself. He cheated on Johnny with the same man the whole time they'd been together. After Johnny confessed he was infected with the virus, this caused the young man to come from behind the wall. He was a tall, dark skin man just like Johnny himself.

"I fucking knew it! Who is he?" Johnny questioned trying to fight the tears that were swelling in his eye ducts.

"That's Charles," Kareem admitted. It was no point of lying; he was already caught red handed.

"Charles, did you know he had a boyfriend?" Johnny asked him clenching his jaws in between his words.

"No, I didn't know." Charles was telling the truth. He wasn't aware that Kareem was involved with another man. Although they always had unprotected sex, he couldn't help but to think he was the one who'd given Kareem HIV, and Kareem gave it to Johnny.

"He has given me HIV!" Johnny said, pointing Kareem's own 9mm at him.

"Johnny you're not thinking straight." Kareem was inching himself near to remove the gun out his hands.

"Back the fuck up nigga!" Johnny said aiming at Kareem's head.

"Now Charles, answer me."

"Yes, I knew because I gave it to him!" Charles admitted giving Kareem HIV which Kareem never knew. This made Johnny see red and he pulled the trigger putting two rounds into Charles' chest and blood splattered all over the kitchen walls.

"AHHHHHHH!" Kareem screamed like a bitch, but if he'd only known what was coming next. He opened the door and ran to his truck but Johnny was quicker than lighting. Pow! Pow! He shot Kareem twice in the back before hurriedly pulling off. This was the rise to Johnny's heartless attitude when he'd gotten away with his first double homicide.

Finally coming back to reality, he continued to look at himself in the mirror before having a nervous breakdown. He was losing a significant amount of weight.

"I FUCKING HATE MYSELF!" he screamed balling up his fist and punching the glass mirror. His new worker, Percy overheard him and knocked on the door,

"Boss you alright?" Percy peeped his head in to find Johnny holding his bloody fist.

"Oh shit! You're bleeding." He rushed to help Johnny wrap his fist but knowing that blood could be one of the ways to contract HIV, Johnny pulled back.

"Get the fuck away from me!" Johnny yelled.

"Ok. I'm just tryna help!" Percy held his hands out trying to help Johnny control himself. He just stood in the doorway watching Johnny act out. Something was truly bothering him.

"GET THE FUCK OUT!"

"You ain't got to tell me twice." Percy closed the door behind himself.

Johnny finally calmed down, grabbed his cell and left out to go to the warehouse. He was speeding up Jefferson unaware that the State boys were waiting to catch someone breaking the law. They got behind Johnny flashing the red light.

"Shit!" Johnny said as he gripped the steering wheel with both hands in front of him. He didn't need to be caught by no State Trooper. They didn't work for him doing crooked shit like the Detroit Police did.

"Evening sir. Can I see your license and registration please?"

"Ok," Johnny said reaching for the information in the glove compartment. He was fluttering through the papers and came across his luger. He wasn't going to kill this man because he was legal and he had absolutely nothing to hide. Finally, after shuffling through millions of papers, he found his registration and handed both pieces of information to the officer out his warm sweaty palms.

"Here you go, sir."

"Thanks." The officer looked down at the name and noticed he was the Johnny that everyone was talking about in the streets.

"Oh, you're that Johnny dude." Johnny just shrugged his shoulders, unaware of how he knew him. He was so big in the streets; this officer could extort him.

"Yea, that's me!" Johnny flashed a fake smile.

"Yes, well I'm going to let you go this time as a warning. But listen to me, I want to work for you so here is my number. Shoot me a call. I'll be down to shoot some pool and talk some business." The officer tore off a piece of paper, scribbled his number on it and handed it to Johnny.

"Alright thanks!" Johnny said as he pulled off.

"Whew, that was close."

Johnny reached his warehouse within 15 minutes after that run down with the cop. When he pulled up, Scar was already there waiting outside leaning up against his car. He flicked his cigar in the snow putting out the cigarette.

"This better be fucking good! Dragging me out of bed on Christmas Eve," Johnny said opening the door to the warehouse. The female workers were bagging the product as usual. He led Scar into his office before closing the door behind them.

"Man, I got some pussy waiting on me. Trust me, I don't want to be out here myself. So, check out this footage your dad had. You won't believe what you see." Scar gave the camera to Johnny.

"What do you want me to do? It seems like your mind is already made up!" Kairo questioned.

"Confess and set your family free!" Johnny Sr. said.

"Ok, ok, ok I killed her! I killed that bitch!" Kairo confessed.

Johnny watched the remainder of the video and began clenching his jaw. Then it was starting to click in his head. Kairo may have wanted to kill his sister because of Malachi.

"See, I was there the entire time she confessed. That's how I know."

"Alright, I'll handle this. You can be dismissed."

Scar left his office at once while Johnny poured him a glass of Dulce and lit up a cigar. He didn't give a damn about speeding up the AIDS process. He already knew he had AIDS once the medication was no longer working. Johnny sat back in his chair and laughed. He laughed so long he began to cough from inhaling the smoke from the cigar.

"Mm, mmm, mm, that bitch Kairo. I knew I should have killed her when I had the chance."

SNITCHES AND DITCHES

*C*lick! Click!

The sound of Delano clicking the suppressor on the gun while pulling up to Scar's residence. He sat across the street on Webb Ave. for 15 minutes and waited patiently for Scar to arrive. He pulled down his black robber mask and got ready to exit his car when Scar finally arrived 5 minutes later at the same time as a woman driving a Jeep Cherokee. Delano waited until Scar got comfortable and settled in first before he decided to make his move.

He picked the back window to sneak through since the room was empty with the door closed. Using his window seal cutter, he lifted the window carefully making sure not to draw any attention to himself. He realized he would have to do a double homicide tonight because witnesses ended up in ditches too. As Delano approached the hallway, he could hear the faint moans of a woman being pleasured coming from upstairs. This attracted him to walk upstairs quietly, making sure not to let the floorboards creak.

"Uuuuhhhh," the woman moaned. The closer Delano got to the room, the louder she became. He finally reached the room they were in and

saw the woman on top of Scar riding his dick like he was a horse. Delano swung the door open, catching the woman off guard. She looked back and he let two shots go.

POW! POW! The bullets landed through her spinal cord, killing her instantly. Blood splattered all over the bed, the walls, and Scar's face.

"What the fuck!" Scar yelled, throwing the dead woman off him and reaching for his gun on the side of him.

POW!

"AGHHHH." The bullet pierced through Scar's arm causing him to bleed over his 1000-count thread sheets.

"What the fuck you know about Cali's death?" Delano asked, aiming the gun in Scar's face hoping to cause intimidation. It worked, because Scar pissed himself. He didn't see this day coming. He knew Johnny would send his men after him.

"I-I-I don't know shit!" Scar said, stuttering with his hands up in the air.

"Bitch, let me jog your memory!" Delano hit Scar in the face with the barrel of the gun.

"Please! I swear I don't know!" he lied.

"You're lying nigga! Get your sorry ass up."

"Where you gone take me? I don't know nothing! Please don't kill me! Please don't kill me!" He pleaded for his life.

"Fuck it," Delano said before squeezing the trigger twice. *POW! POW!*

After that, Delano returned home as if he didn't just body a nigga. He found Kairo sitting in the living room snuggled up in her oversized tan sweater hanging off the shoulder. She was drinking a glass of red wine and Delano knocked that glass out her hand causing the wine glass to shatter.

"Why you do that?" Kairo started to get angry. She got up to make another glass of wine.

"Don't be drinking that shit while you're pregnant. I want my baby healthy!"

"Well at this fucking rate, I'm not sure if the baby is even going to have a father, you keep roaming the streets like you do." Kairo was drunk and emotional. She knew this was Delano's life before she took his last name.

"You are fucking lucky yo' ass is drunk. I oughta punch yo' ass in the fucking throat!" he threatened, and Kairo didn't take that lightly. She was now in Delano's face.

"Oh yea, nigga? Do it then!"

Shit escalated between them so quickly that Malachi had to come and pull Kairo out the room. She was upset that Delano left her often for the streets. She thought being pregnant would slow him down and keep him out the streets, but she was wrong.

"I'm out here trying to protect yo' ass and my family! Man, you better get out my face with that bullshit!" Delano said before taking a cold beer out the fridge and sitting down on the black leather, L-shaped sectional.

"Bitches be so ungrateful these days," Delano mumbled to himself before taking a sip of his Heineken. He hated Kairo didn't understand his reasons or actions. It was almost like she didn't trust him. He turned the TV off and went upstairs to apologize to his wife.

Kairo was sitting down in front of her vanity brushing her hair into a wrap, watching Delano walk into the room. She was still pissed at him for ditching her on his birthday. He closed the door behind him and decided to tell Kairo what happened that night.

"We need to talk." Delano approached her, taking the brush out her hand.

"About?"

"You want to know why I had to leave early tonight?"

"Why? I mean, why would I want to know?"

"Well for starters, let me apologize because I should have told you about Johnny finding out about Cali's death."

"What? How?" Kairo turned around and this gained her full attention.

"Well, I killed the man before he could talk," Delano said.

"Who?"

"Some weak ass nigga who tried to talk," Delano admitted.

"Well thanks for telling me."

"There is something else I want to tell you, but you have to promise not to ever tell anyone."

"Who the fuck I'm gone tell Delano?"

"Kairo!"

"Alright, alright. Damn," she said, slipping into her sexy purple negligee.

"Never mind," Delano said, changing his mind about telling her about his secret. He wasn't sure how she was going to react to him finding out that Johnny Sr. was his biological father. The news still didn't settle right with him. He still thought the DNA test was fabricated so he decided not to say anything.

"What's the matter baby?" she asked, getting into bed with him.

"Nothing baby. Did you find out what's going to happen to your condo?" Delano asked to change the subject.

"Well what are you going to do about my condo?" Kairo asked. Although they were now married and living together again under one roof, Delano was still responsible for all the damages he'd caused.

"I'll give you 20 grand tomorrow. Let's just relax and enjoy the rest of my birthday."

Delano leaned over to kiss Kairo's shoulders, pulling up her purple negligee. He inserted two fingers and fingered her pussy to a satisfying orgasm. She gripped the sheets moaning and pulled on her own nipples. His fingers increased in speed as she grinded on them like it was a hard penis inside her. Delano pulled her hair as he put in his rock-hard penis from the side. Her moans turned him on and encouraged him to thrust deeper inside her warm cave.

Boom! Boom!

"What the fuck is that noise?" Delano said while he was mid-stroke inside Kairo. She grabbed the covers and looked at him.

"Man, I'll be right back." Delano slipped on his boxers and wrapped a towel around his waist, picking up his heat off the nightstand. In the distance he could hear glass being shattered, sounding like his car windows were being busted. He ran down the stairs and to the garage where he saw both of cars were set on fire, but he forgot to close the garage behind him.

"What the fuck!" Delano yelled, grabbing the fire extinguisher and putting the fire out. Kairo came rushing down the stairs to see what all the commotion was going on downstairs.

Ding Dong!

The doorbell rang causing Delano to freeze in his steps. *Who the fuck could be at my door at 1 am?* he thought, leaving to go check the door. Malachi finally woke up from inhaling the smoke that filled his room and came rushing down the stairs as well. The smoke detectors sounded throughout the whole house once the smoke filled the entire garage. Malachi grabbed the other fire extinguisher and helped put out the fires.

"Dad, what is going on?" Malachi asked.

Ding Dong!

"Nothing. Stay right there."

Delano clicked his gun while slowly walking to the door. He touched the doorknob, twisted it, and opened it. He was face-to-face with a silencer aimed directly at his head.

"Hello, Delano."

To be continued…

A WORD FROM the Author

Hello Love Bugs. Thank you for tuning in with me again. I promise each book will get juicier. Stay tuned for *Addicted to a Detroit Savage 3* coming soon. I want to encourage every one of you that is afraid to chase your dream, don't be afraid. Sometimes all it takes is faith to get you started. If you are an aspiring writer and want to practice your writing skills, add April Nicole Erotic Short Stories on Facebook. You also need support!!!! Support is the hardest thing to find, but one of the easiest things to give. Make sure to like The Love Bug Lounge or add April Nicole's Readers Group for a chance to win prizes or to write a review. Let me know what you think.

*April Nicole on Facebook

*Aprilnicole_2012 on Instagram

- April Nicole

ABOUT APRIL NICOLE,

. . .

INSPIRED BY HER FAVORITE AUTHORESS, Zane, April hopes to become very successful in her writing career. She graduated from King High school in 2012 and continued her academic journey at Davenport University, where she later decided that writing was the path she wanted to take. On January 27th she released her first urban novel, *Addicted to a Detroit Savage*, which gained popularity around Detroit.

A NOTE FROM THE AUTHOR

Hello Love Bugs!!!

I hope you have enjoyed reading the story just as much as I did writing it. This is my very first novel, so I wanted to you to be a part of this experience. I want to encourage you to follow your dream, no matter what may come up against you. In life we go through many trials, some greater than others, but no matter what, stick in there. You must achieve what YOU believe in. Stay tuned friends, pt 2 is coming soon.

Until next time, chao.

ABOUT THE AUTHOR

April Nicole Marie, is a loving, devoted mother who was born and raised in the city of Detroit better known as the "Motor City." She began her writing career at the age of 13, traveling and winning oratorical speeches around the city.

Inspired by her favorite Authoress "Zane" she began to write her own erotica short stories in high school, sharing them amongst her class mates. April graduated from M. L. King High school in 2012, and later attended Davenport University majoring in Business Administration. Now April is currently employed as a Credit Specialist at a well-known corporation, and plan on pursuing her writing career full time. If you ever want drama, entertainment, and a thrill look no further. She is here to bring that heat. You will constantly be at the edge of your seat wanting to know what's going to happen next.

Stay Connected:

Follow me on Facebook "April Nicole's Erotic Short Stories," or if you have any questions or suggestions please email me at
aprilnicolemarie@gmail.com.

CPSIA information can be obtained
at www.ICGtesting.com
Printed in the USA
LVHW041657061120
670968LV00006B/1021